# Groovy People

REGI NELSON

GROOVY PEOPLE
Copyright © 2020 Regi Nelson
First Edition

First originally published by Newman Springs Publishing 2020


Newman Springs Publishing
320 Broad Street
Red Bank, NJ 07701


ISBN 978-1-64801-401-7 (Paperback)
ISBN 978-1-64801-402-4 (Digital)


Printed in the United States of America

To my son and grandkids.
Never give up on your dreams.

When Kelly called, Max was very busy doing financial statements and inventory for the upcoming quarterly reports. When she heard the urgency in Kelly's voice, Max stopped everything she was doing to take a seat and listen.

While Max was driving over to Kelly's place, she kept replaying the conversation over and over in her head. She still could not figure out what was so important that Kel needed to see her right away.

"Hello?"

"Hi, Max. This is Kel."

"Girl, I know who this is. What's going on?"

"I need to talk to you."

"You sound serious. Okay, I'm all ears."

"No, *really* talk to you. Can you get away? Come by now?"

"Yeah, Kel. What's up?"

"I'll tell you everything when you get here."

Kelly hung up, and Max reviewed all the possible files she had in her mind on Kelly that might trigger a reaction of this magnitude. She thought about Kelly's mom who was getting up in age but, for the most part, was pretty healthy. Kelly and her mother were really close and have always had a great relationship, so Max could understand Kelly's reaction if something was wrong with her mom. Max remembered that time when Ms. LeBeau broke her fingernail so close to the quick. It bled and hurt her so bad, and she cried. She called Kelly sobbing on the phone, trying to tell Kelly what happened, just sniffling and slinging snot.

"Mom, what's wrong?"

"Kelly, baby, I'm bleeding. My finger is cut, and it really hurts."

"Mom, listen to me. Hang up the phone and unlock the door. I'm on my way."

Kelly called 911 and sent the paramedics to her mother's house. She told them her mother is elderly and that she cut herself and is in a lot of pain.

"Ma'am, how did your mom cut herself?" the robotic voice on the other end of the line asked.

"I don't know. She called me crying and in serious pain. Look, are you going to help or not?"

"Calm down, ma'am," the unaffected voice requested of Kelly. "Where is the cut?"

"Look, damn it, don't tell me to calm down. You calm down when your mother is bleeding and suffering! I don't know where the cut is. I pay taxes, my mother pays taxes, and if she is in need of your services for once in her many years of paying your wages, then she should receive that service. As quickly and friendly and thoroughly as possible. Her address is 438 Clintock Road, Norcross." *Click*. Kelly hung up.

Kelly only lived a couple of miles from her mother, although they were divided by city limits. Kelly found a nice, clean, and quiet place for her mother that would only take her a few moments to get to if she needed to check on her mom, get a good meal, or cry on her shoulder. Kelly did make sure it was just far enough away to limit easy access so she could have a little privacy and the freedom she needed to be her own person. She hadn't forgotten how suffocating and possessive her mother could be about her only daughter. She only lived a ten-minute drive away by highway, and Kelly could get there within seventeen minutes by surface street if necessary. She knew every shortcut, side street, and back way possible to her mother's duplex. No traffic jam, detour, or disaster could keep her from arriving at her mother's home in record time if she needed to get there in a hurry. Right now, she needed to get there in a hurry. Kelly arrived approximately four minutes behind the paramedics, and their response time is usually three to five minutes.

Ms. LeBeau was thinking either the paramedics were slow—although she actually thought the paramedics popped up out of nowhere after she hung up the phone with Kelly—or Scottie must have beamed Kelly down because she arrived lightning quick.

Ms. LeBeau watched her daughter as she hurled herself from the car and began chastising and inquiring in her usual fussy and overreacting way where her mother was concerned. Kelly was talking in warp speed. You could see the paramedics looking at her with that blank, empty stare like you see on TV when the bubblehead blonde talks on forever about nothing and her audience is waiting for the lights to come on and her brain cells to connect. If only she would pause to breathe so they could interject an answer to at least one of her many questions. One paramedic thought he would have to cease treatment on Ms. LeBeau and render CPR or oxygen to Kelly because it looked as if she was going to pass out from overexertion. Finally, she inhaled. The paramedic explained the situation with her mom.

"Your mom split the bed of her nail when she broke the tip off. It's not that bad. It just hurts like heck when that happens. Nothing life-threatening," he cajoled Kelly.

"Well, why was she bleeding so profusely?" Kelly ignored his teasing.

"It wasn't exactly profusely. But the blood does flow rather steadily when you break the skin there, and it does hurt," he explained.

Kelly began regaining her ability to process information as she settled down. "What should she do now?"

"We cleaned and dressed it pretty good, so now all she has to do is keep it dry and keep that finger elevated and pointed up. That will eliminate blood from rushing to that area and causing the finger to throb with pain. If she can take acetaminophen or ibuprofen, that should be enough to stop the pain as necessary. If she gets worse or experiences a reaction, go to the emergency room immediately. Otherwise, follow up with your own physician in a couple of days. Get that dressing changed or removed. Otherwise, my prognostication is she'll be back to her usual self in no time."

He smiled at her in that way so many men respond to Kelly, flirting although slightly intimidated by her beauty yet respecting the strength she exudes while, at the same time, emitting her femininity and innocence.

Kelly recognized the move and, this time, was a bit flattered. But she kept her cool as she smilingly thought about his attempt to impress her with his technical knowledge. Cute though basic. Who didn't know what acetaminophen was? He gets bonus points for *prognostication* and a couple of cool points for being able to get her attention regardless of how elementary the approach. In fact, that was probably the attracting element. She smiled back and thanked him for tending to her mother so professionally and kindly.

Ms. LeBeau watched the interaction with pride as she so often observed this reaction from people who come in contact with her daughter. He, like so many others, instantly fell in love though they don't immediately understand the attraction—men, women, and children alike. They must feel the genuine sincerity and love of Kelly's soul. She also remembers the flip side of this child of hers. Kelly is the most extreme child she has ever seen. The depths of the anger that she spews when she's forced to bring out Samantha—Kelly's evil twin—is equally as intense as her love. Most cannot remain angry or hate Kelly for as long she maintains her hurt and anger once she is vexed. Many have failed trying to regain that loving, fun-filled, trusting side after forcing her to abandon it. Mrs. LeBeau just shook her head and tried to hold in her laughter as the paramedics left.

"What are you laughing at, missy?" Kelly exclaimed to her mom jokingly.

"You just look a little exhausted and deflated after your crusade to save my finger. Sending the paramedics, going off on the paramedics. Child, you know, you can get excited. Are *you* all right now?" Mrs. LeBeau joked back.

"Well, you were the one who called me babbling and huffing in pain about your finger being sliced off," Kelly said sarcastically, making air quotes. "All pitiful and everything. That's not even a cut!"

"It felt like it had been sliced off, and blood was gushing allover"

Kelly cut her mom off "Gushing?" as she looked at her mom sideways with objection. They both commenced to cracking up until tears welled in their eyes. Mrs. LeBeau forgot to keep her finger up, and blood rushed to the tip of it, and it began throbbing just as the paramedic said it would.

Mrs. LeBeau's body tightened with pain and her face winced. "Oooh!" she cried out.

"Are you okay, Mom?" The laughter was gone in an instant, and concern consumed Kelly's face.

"Yes, child," Mrs. LeBeau responded patronizingly and chuckled. "But I better get some *acetaminophen* and keep this finger up."

Max didn't know what Kelly would do if something happened to her mother. Max was afraid to even think any further on those possibilities. She could not figure for the life of her what could be troubling Kelly. She thought Kelly always had it so good. Three big brothers who were crazy about their little sister and spoiled her as much as her mom and dad did. A mother who is super sweet and they are best friends. Brains and beauty, and men who wanted to do nothing but take care of her. A flock of family and friends who simply love her to no end.

"What could possibly be troubling Kelly?" Max thought out loud as she turned the corner of Kelly's posh neighborhood in Stone Mountain.

Kelly had recently moved there a little less than two years ago after receiving her promotion to chief engineer. She'd been with Boeing Industries, a high-powered company that leads the nation producing electronic devices, for nearly ten years. Kelly stayed in college straight through the completion of her master's degree in mechanical engineering. After graduating from Howard University, she was recruited by one of California's top engineering companies where she stayed for two years until she was offered a senior position at Boeing. She has been there ever since, steadily climbing the corporate ladder because she is good at her job. Kelly's first year was one of her most productive years. She redesigned the horizontal stabilizer, a piece on the tail used to improve the dynamic stability of aircrafts and keep them flying straight. She made it more efficient, less costly to produce and longer lasting. The company saved and profited an additional eight million that year, and to show their appreciation, immediately offered her a position heading the production branch at the company.

Kelly knew that in this business, all that mattered were the numbers and the next new innovative product. She continued to work hard and impress the right people and to her surprise, though well-deserved, was offered the chief position after the retirement of Johnson Elders. She was surprised for several reasons: one, no black person has ever had an opportunity at the position, let alone a black female. Also, there was a white male lined up for the position, who everyone thought pretty much had it in the bag. Kelly didn't think she was getting the position, but she hoped anyone except that jerk would get it. He always gave Kelly the blues on one issue or another, and she knew if he was ever in a position of management over her, he'd give her hell. The biggest shock of all came from the fact that Johnson Elders recommended her. This surprised Kelly because they had a run-in a few years prior, and although they kept a professional relationship, she didn't think he would ever be a key player in her professional advancement.

John Elders started as chief engineer thirty-eight years ago when he was about three or four years younger than Kelly when she first started. He was a hard-nosed guy who ran a seriously tight ship but was pretty fair in his management practices and business dealings. He could be real ruthless if ever crossed or if there was a bid for a job that could bring the company more business and profit and more accolades for him. Due to his intense combatant tendencies, he not only got what he wanted but also never shied away from the opportunity to punish those who interfered or tried to hinder him from accomplishing his goals. Kelly never imagined she would get too far up the corporate ladder at Boeing for those very reasons. When they had their incident, she cursed him up one side and down the other. If he could have fired her then, he would have, but he knew how the CEOs felt about their new engineers, especially those who proved they could bring profit to the company. That side that Ms. LeBeau had so regularly pleaded with her daughter to control and "have greater patience when dealing with those white folks" had surfaced in full battle gear and refused to retreat until completely out of ammunition.

Kelly received a note attached to one of her proposals that was so filled with red marks and corrections that it looked as though the paper was bleeding. Mr. Elders corrected her literary style and made reference to her being an incompetent writer and using bad grammar. It was unfortunate that Johnson's view of Black universities was that of an institution created to disseminate degrees to less qualified persons who couldn't cut it at a "real" college.

To the misfortune of America, this view is adapted by many persons, including some black ones, but founded on no identifiable facts. He has been given no reason to believe as he does, and he has never made any inquiries or done research to validate this stereotypical misconception. When Kelly finished with him, there was no research left to be done, no questions left unanswered, and no room for misunderstanding.

"Mr. Elders, is there a particular reason why you've marked up my proposal and wrote me this asinine note?"

"Asinine?" Elders huffed and squared himself off as he prepared for this battle, as he so thrived on these type of opportunities. Once again, it was a chance to deflate an overrated rookie who was full of themself and send them scurrying home in tears. "I'll tell you what's asinine. Accrediting these fly-by-night, incompetent facilities and selling degrees to any Joe who decides they want to circumvent working hard for a real education. Then they come down here pretending to be qualified engineers, writing up proposals and trying to fool the board of directors into believing they have ideas that are of some value to this company."

Kelly was seething. She didn't know which issue to address first. Kelly grew three inches in stature right before Elders eyes, wound up her sistah neck, and called on her Maker to spare this fool her total wrath and bless her tongue to articulate the facts as they apply to this situation. She prayed to dismiss the desire to inform him of the laws that needed better enforcing to inhibit procreation between relatives and the rearing of Montana, log-cabin-living, postal-crazed hell spawns. She was proud of her alma mater and knew anyone with half the common sense of a flea realized the full ability of historical black universities to competitively educate anyone who desires a good education, equal to that of any Ivy League. There was no doubt of the quality of the education she received as well as her ability to exhibit those qualities.

Without as much as a flinch, Kelly told him, "Black colleges have been educating black people, and anyone else who was interested, with a success rate far exceeding these so-called acceptable colleges. They are accredited, and justifiably so, since they had to teach their students to be twice as good to get only half the credit. Thanks to America and her disparate tendencies, they had to prepare their students and equip them with skills and knowledge several levels above the average learned individual. People like yourself stereotype and disqualify on mere assumptions, sustained by no intelligent thought or experience to confound those tired-ass views. Then the one time an act of congress forces you to deal with a product of those institutions you know nothing about, they're crowned 'prince different from the rest of them' by folk like yourself. No, they aren't different from the rest of us. They're part of the norm. The majority of us are free-willed, rational-thinking, hardworking persons. We just don't have the power of the media to frequently display your trailer park counterparts as you do our people. The knucklehead you so eagerly adopt as the average black person is the one who is different, and there would probably be even less of those types if the struggle to get a small slice of what America has to offer was not so unbalanced."

Kelly exhaled, but only for a brief second. There were two other territories she had to tread. Before Elders could digest, get angry, or respond, she began again.

"And as far as purchasing a degree is concerned, there are more shops and persons who look like you that sell reports and thesis, pay off professors, and get investigated for scandals of selling test scores than any black person or university I've heard ever about. The best kept-secret of paying less and receiving an equal or better education has slipped into the mainstream and many nonblacks are taking advantage of those wonderful programs. Now if you have encountered a black engineer pretending to be qualified, I bet she didn't graduate in the top ten rank of her class. I bet she was not recruited by several major companies while still in undergraduate school. I bet her skills were questionable because she didn't work ten times as diligently just to get an interview to let the facts speak for themselves. If she did try to circumvent getting an education and true ability, spending six straight years mastering her field would not have been the most intelligent way to achieve your shameful suggestion. If she did not know how to write, her award-winning thesis would not have sparked a program that includes courses offering specialized certificates in mechanical engineering. She would not have been recruited or promoted, and this proposal would not be upstairs with the directors where they are considering setting up a budget for a pilot program to adopt her 'brainless ideas.'"

Kelly did an about-face, clicked her heels as steady as any soldier with confidence and military bearing, and walked away. Everything became a blur.

She wanted to look back and see his expression; see if she could possibly get some reading of her future from his face. She didn't really need to see him to know her demise. She had witnessed enough of Johnson Elders to know her resume would need to get circulated real soon. She had to work fast and start submitting them to several companies before her name became a four-letter word in the industry. Her mother had warned her about that temper of hers, but she couldn't let that man treat her any way he wanted.

She could not let him get away with such evil and face herself every day or him, for that matter, because he would not stop there. As Kelly's vision began to focus, she noticed she passed by one of the CEO's administrative assistant who had apparently overheard everything. Ian had a smirk on his face that indicated both amusement and fear. Amused that someone finally gave the old pompous bag of wind the lashing he deserved. Fear for Kelly's future and of going into the same room with Elders to have him sign off on the file he was bringing to John's office. He knew Elders was going to blow, and he didn't want to be anywhere near the line of fire. Kelly went straight to her office and began taking down her personal effects, clearing her office out for what she thought was sure to come.

*What was I thinking?* she thought to herself. *Everything does not have to be said. That was my boss. I have too good of a job to throw it away for some ignorant person's view. He's not the only person who feels that way and certainly not the last idiot I'll run into throughout my career. I played right into his trap. Lose my career trying to prove my worth to someone whose opinion doesn't even matter and will remain unchanged nonetheless. Oh well, can't unscramble those eggs. Just try to practice better restraint next time. If there is a next time. I don't know what's gonna happen with my career now.*

Elders stood in his same spot, in his same position, in shock. She left him squared off for battle, and he remained in that stance. Too proud to slump in defeat and certainly too mighty to retreat. His frozen shock mostly stemmed from realizing she, this wet-behind-the-ear rookie, had the audacity to approach him with disdain. Then have the last word and walk away. Not *walk*—*saunter* away. How dare she? That was his style—leave 'em stunned.

When Ian muscled up the courage to walk into the office, John was smiling. Ian was sure he'd already conjured some form of torture for Kelly's destruction.

John was actually a bit amused; he was downright tick-led. Ian decided the signature could wait, and he hightailed it out of there, picked up his coat and keys, and grabbed Kelly. He was taking her on a long lunch break, far from the office, at least three miles away, in a setting with television so they could watch for live breaking news. Ian was sure John Elders had snapped and was on the verge of going postal. That sinister laugh he witnessed was more than he needed to confirm John had completely lost it.

Kelly laughed at Ian as they sat down at the bar of their favorite little getaway. Ian had introduced it to her just two months after she joined Boeing Industries.

Ian took an immediate liking to Kelly, and the usual trial period to earn your way to Second Chance was waived. Second Chance is a posh little bar and restaurant with a band that plays from lunch until the end of happy hour. It's located between the business district and a slightly less desirable part of town. It's a dark, well-maintained build-ing with few windows, low light, and lots of mirrors. It has a circular bar with several television monitors for the watching pleasure and entertainment of those who fail to be completely fulfilled by the talent and stories of the bar-tender. The very talented in-house band could strike up a rendition of almost any pop, R&B, or easy listening selec-tion of the last four decades. It was not out of the ordinary for a downright head-shaking, hip-swinging party to break out in the middle of the lunch hour. Sometimes only easy listening would consume the lunch hour, and Kelly and Ian would just dance in one another's arms, talking endlessly about anything, everything, nothing. At times, others would join them or they'd be out there alone the entire lunch.

Second Chance has a very relaxing atmosphere, but it's almost like a secret club. If you're new there, everyone knows it and wants to know who you are and who invited you. It's as if the music stops when the new face enters, and the moment freezes while everyone waits for the person to be cleared before things resume. It's the kind of place you can go to and impress your friends yet feel enough at home to relax and enjoy yourself. Once you've been there, you're hooked, and the people miss you when you stay away too long.

Today, Kelly and Ian sat at the bar while Ian watched for a broadcast interruption with a special bulletin from the beautiful upscale building of Boeing Industries in Uptown Atlanta. They discussed the events of the morning. Ian was genuinely afraid for Kelly. He was certain her position at Boeing was history, and he really didn't believe she'd ever have an opportunity at another prestigious firm or position in her field. His bigger concern stemmed from the loss he would suffer when she was gone. He had become very close and dependent on Kelly's presence within a short period of knowing one another, and he could not fathom the thought of not having contact with her every day. Men and women alike made assumptions about Kelly and Ian's relationship and their personal integrity and sincerity. Their closeness disturbed and intrigued many at their company and in their social circle.

Women routinely made bold advances at Ian. Since he usually didn't respond to their overt gestures, it wasn't long before they decided he was a conceited jerk. He would always say, "If they're trying that hard to give it away, it must not be worth much. You rarely see someone tossing out anything of value." Ian is about six feet three inches with wavy hair with a close fade on the sides. He is slender, good-looking, and a rather jaunty dresser. He looked good in his clothes and knew it, not to the point of irritation but only to the extent of making sure he keeps himself in order. Kelly knows how Ian feels about her, and she equally adores him and their relationship. She knows how genuine and loving he is, and she cherishes all they have developed over time.

Ian knew everything there was to know about Boeing Industries and its mission and kept close watch on the competition. He was the eyes and ears of the company. His executive, as well as the company itself, would be hard-pressed without him around.

Anytime there was a presentation or project coming up, he had all the required materials available and prepared long before his boss realized he would need those items. Kelly would venture to say Ian is the best at his position, at least as far as she had seen. There was no doubt in her mind that given the technical skill, Ian could run circles around any engineer in the department. The bond in their relationship probably stemmed from their common char-acteristics. Kelly constantly had to prove herself and her abilities while her colleagues' training and experience was never questioned. Being a young black woman in a field dominated by men, she knew every milestone would be an upward climb. She experienced racism, sexism, and many other isms. Ian was not foolish enough to believe his struggle came remotely close to the many hundreds of years of discrimination and mistreatment black people have been forced to endure, but being gay has its trials and tribulations. They both have to deal with prejudices and stereotypes. Every day is a battle to avoid being prejudged on their abilities and the type of person they are.

This current hurdle is minuscule in comparison to those Kelly have encountered trying to achieve success. Growing up a black child in the ghetto, so many seductions to things that could inhibit her future presented itself to her. At age nine and ten, she had to resist the temptation to steal along with the rest of the other kids. This resistance came a little easier than others because she knew her mom would go apeshit crazy. That would be her last day of sunshine until she was twenty-one years old.

The teen years introduced ditching school, cigarette smoking, and sex. There were times when Kelly almost gave into this bait, but she had so many brothers that very little went on in their neighborhood that they didn't know about. Kelly knew they would kick her butt royally and massacre everyone else involved in helping her go astray.

That reality deterred most persons from involving Kelly in their charades.

Sometimes her brothers' interference bothered Kelly. But her other alternative was for them to tell her mother, and Kelly was sure she'd die a slow, agonizing death if her mom got a hold of any bad information. Yep, she'd definitely kill her if she even thought Kelly was doing wrong in school or foolish enough to release her pride and power to some "snot-nosed, pimple-faced, undeserving testosterone carrier with no morals or respect for himself or you, or he wouldn't have even tried to have sex with you in the first place."

Kelly loved all her brothers, and deep down, she appreciated everything they did for her. Much of their preaching was hypocritical, but they always told her society views things differently for girls than boys.

"If I have sex young and have a lot of girls, I'm becoming a man. If you have a bunch of guys, you're becoming a whore, whether or not you have sex with them. Someone or something will constantly remind you of it until you begin to act just as they perceive you," her oldest brother, Ted, informed her.

"Not only that, to make things worse, the one who told you he loved you is usually the one starting the rumors and hurting your feelings," her brother Mack added to the soup they were brewing.

Then came Dexter with his two cents. "No, the worst part is someone will start rumors and talk about you even when nothing happens. And they will lie."

"Imagine that! The only redeeming factor on that issue is you know the truth for yourself and most others also know when you carry yourself in a respectful manner. Besides, only you know what you've done, who you are, and where you're going," echoed her oldest brother again.

"And where is that?" Mack led the chorus as they prepared to close the conversation with their ritual announcement.

"To college to major in engineering, graduate with honors, make big bank, and take us out for serious eats every month," they all sang out in unison and laughed every time.

Kelly did just that. They knew she would. Kelly was a wizard in mathematics. "A badass in math," her brother would say. She tutored all of them on most of their schoolwork, even the older ones, when she was just a little thing.

They toughened her up pretty good. She was thick-skinned, and she could take a joke and issue out some pretty good ones as well. She could hold her own when someone insisted on making her fight them. She didn't like to fight, but out of the whole three fights in her lifetime, she mopped the floor with the individual. She was taught to never let anyone put their hands on her with intent to harm her and get away with it. Her brothers never hit Kelly, but she didn't know they would not hit her until she was almost twenty-one years old. She was graduating from her undergraduate program, and they were all together, eating and reminiscing, when Kelly brought up the subject. She told them they scared her into being a good student and staying away from the influence of the neighborhood.

With all her brothers' caring, lectures, and tough love and her mother's speeches, talks, and embraces, nothing could prepare her for the hurt she would experience when she finally fell for that special guy.

How it hurt. Oh, it hurt so badly. Kelly would have preferred getting gut-punched by her brother, the Canadian league football star. She cried, and she cursed. She cursed, and she cried. She hated him, but she loved him so much. Why couldn't he stay in DC and work until Kelly finished her master's degree?

Kevin was so good to her; she just knew they'd be together for all time. They were made for each other, Kelly and Kevin. Everyone always commented on what a perfect couple they were. Her classmates used to tease them and sing an old grammar school rhyme: "Kelly and Kevin sitting in a tree, K-I-S-S-I-N-G. First comes love, then comes marriage, then comes the baby in the baby carriage." That embarrassed Kelly, but she also figured they were right. That's how things were supposed to be. Finish high school, go to college, meet your love, marry him, have a family, and live happily ever after. Of course, you have your ups and downs—everyone does. She wasn't that naïve to the trials of loving and living with someone, but love and commitment will bring you through those pits of life. Her parents did it. She was from a family with strong family values and generations of sticking together and raising their families to do the same.

Kelly sure did not intend to be the one to break that tradition. Unfortunately, Kevin had other plans. He blasted Kelly's fantasy of having kids and giving them all names that began with *K* and being the K-Family because Kevin's last name is Kincaid. How could he do this? It was all so perfect. She had everything worked out. She would give new meaning to KKK. Kevin and Kelly Kincaid. Now what is she supposed to do?

Of course, he played the role, pretending they would still be together; that distance wouldn't cause a strain on their relationship.

"Baby, absence will just make the heart grow fonder."

"Kevin, that only applies if it's a separation for a brief period, not relocating two thousand miles away," Kelly said, not impressed with his rationale.

"We need a little space between us for a while. We've been under each other for over two years now."

There it was, Kelly thought, the real reason he wants to leave. He wanted to get away from her; get some air. Probably another girl.

"What kind of space? People who love each other don't separate and have trials of living apart. I thought you wanted to marry me," she whined.

Kevin did plan to marry Kelly. He meant everything he said to her when they discussed their future. He was more than ready to walk down the aisle last year, but Kelly wanted to start her master's program and get married after she graduated. She didn't want her scholarship and grants to be affected by the marital status. He would also be attached to her loans and bills if they got married while she was actively enrolled and using the funds. Kevin agreed it was a fair compromise and figured they would have more time in their courtship to enjoy each other before taking the plunge and doing the family thing.

Yeah, that would have been best, but something happened since that time. He started feeling smothered and suffocated. His life would be changing and Kevin was scared. But he didn't know why, and he didn't know how to tell Kelly. He thought he didn't really need to tell her because it would pass and they'd be together soon. Michigan was not that far away, and besides, Kelly only had a year left to graduate and they could then start their life. The change would do them both some good, he rationalized. *One year. Yeah, that's enough time to catch my breath and enjoy my life before I make the commitment,* Kevin thought to himself.

"Kelly, I do want to marry you. This change will be good for the both of us. I can go to Michigan, get a job, and get settled, and when you finish school, you can join me and we'll do everything as planned."

"But why Michigan, Kevin? That's so far away, and we never discussed moving there as an option when we talked about our future."

"I know, baby. Sometimes plans change. Everything will work out. You'll see."

Kelly thought to herself, *Here we go again. Same old vague answers, and no real reasons for all these changes and surprises. I'm not getting anywhere on this subject.* Then she said, "I don't know, Kevin. This just doesn't make sense to me, but it appears you have your mind made up."

Kelly gave up. In an effort to change the topic and hopefully change Kevin's mind, she asked him if he wanted some dinner. She knew there were two things Kevin could not resist—her cooking and her loving. She decided to make both temptations extra special that night.

Kevin wished Kelly didn't know his weaknesses because it just made things more difficult. He had to go. There was no alternative, or he'd no longer recognize himself. He was quickly being transformed into everyone's perception of him.

Kelly dotted all the i's and crossed all the t's and didn't miss a single punctuation, especially the exclamation marks. She made serious love to her man. First, she filled him with her favorite recipe, his favorite dish, meatloaf with macaroni and cheese and candied yams on the side, and those super moist walnut brownies they both like so much. After dinner, she helped him with his bath.

It was a sweet, sensuous night. Kelly lit the fireplace, burned some African musk oil that softly scented her place, and lit the house with candles. There were two large candles in the corners of her bedroom and an ocean-scented pillar candle in the bathroom. She ran a lukewarm tub of water and washed Kevin's back when he got in the tub. While Kevin was lathering himself, Kelly climbed into the tub with him. He began washing her body, and they made love right there. Kelly had the most amazing orgasm, and Kevin was so out of breath that he collapsed against the back of the tub. They switched to the shower, washed up again, dried each other off, and went to the kitchen to eat. Stark naked. Kelly knew Kevin liked to look at her body, and she was just as crazy about his. They took their plates to the living room to sit at the fireplace and listen to some soft music. They only ate a few bites before they were all over one another again. It must have been the Brian McKnight CD. It'll get you every time. When they came up for air, Kevin had to go get some ice water. They were both drained and dehydrated. They were panting like gold-medal Olympians in the sex decathlon. They talked and teased each other for a while and then Kelly jumped onto Kevin's back and rode her pony into the bedroom.

It was in this room that she would make the sweetest, most passionate love to the most important man in her life, next to her dad and brothers. She massaged his weary body and rubbed oil over him, paying special attention to his sensitive points. She caressed and kissed his body and sucked his nipples. Then she began to rub oil on herself. All this attention brought Kevin's body back to life, and he finished rubbing the oil over Kelly. Her body opened up and begged for Kevin to enter, and he slid in ever so gently. He was so excited that he had to muster all the strength and concentration he could gather so he wouldn't come too soon. He eased out of her and grabbed her by her butt and legs and slid her down in the bed so he could mas-sage, caress, and talk to her soft spot in a language that only the two of them understood. Kelly moaned and cried out with gratification and tried to backpedal up the bed. It felt so good, but her nerves couldn't take it. She asked for relief, tossed and turned, and suddenly began to convulse. She had no control over the motion of her body. As she wrenched, her back arched, and she squeezed Kevin's head with her thigh. He held on to her, trying to extend her pleasure and suck up the flavor of her womanhood.

While she was coming down, Kevin reentered her body cavity and sent her back up the rollercoaster. She rolled him over onto his back and kissed his now sensitive chest and moved her body up and down his maleness until his toes began to curl. Kevin's body tightened up, and he shouted some expletives as Kelly gave him all her energy. She sat up and moved even faster on his throne. Kevin's legs weakened. He pounded the bed in defeat and continued to rise to meet Kelly's body. Kelly screamed with excitement and surrender. They came together and fell limp into each other's arms. Kelly moved slowly on Kevin, trying to relieve him of all the tension and fluid pressure in his body. They fell asleep hard. Kelly was prepared to give him many more like that too. Anything for her man. Even after the kids were born, Kelly had plans on how to make special nights alone for the two of them.

The following week, Kevin was out of there. Before going over to Kelly's, he stopped by Mona's place to thank her for connecting him with her father to get that job. Of course, this made his transition much smoother, and now all he had to do once he got to Michigan was find a place to stay. Until then, he'd be at Mona's parents the first few weeks but no longer. Kevin didn't want to stay too long, mostly because of one of the comments made by Mona's dad during one of their phone conversations before Kevin had arrived. "Any friend of my daughter's is welcome in our home, and you came highly recommended young man." Kevin could hear the gesture in Mr. Rush's voice but didn't want to acknowledge what he thought was going on.

"Oh, Kevin, it was nothing. Glad to help out a friend. Besides, you're kinda helping me. Getting someone to work for my dad will ease the shock of me not coming to work for him when I graduate. Since our major is the same and you've already graduated, I figure I'd send you as decoy."

"Aha, so you're just using me to pacify Daddy," Kevin said jokingly.

"What are friends for?" Mona asked slyly. They both laughed.

"Well, thanks. Really. I appreciate everything."

Kevin hugged Mona and headed back to Kelly's place with everything packed and stuffed in his little Honda Civic.

Kelly had already been crying before he got there. She was sad and mad. He could have at least waited until Christmas break. It was only three weeks away. Now she would have to spend Christmas without her man. More than anything, she just hated that he was leaving, holiday or not. She did not want that kind of time and space between her and Kevin.

Kevin walked into the bathroom and caught Kelly trying to straighten herself up. She didn't even hear him come in.

"Aw, baby, come on now. Don't cry. Don't make this any harder than it is."

Between tears and sobbing, Kelly said, "I'm sorry, but I just love you so much. It's killing me to watch you go."

"I love you too, baby." Kevin cupped Kelly's face, tilted her chin up, and gave her a reassuring kiss.

Kelly wiped her face and sank her head into Kevin's chest, holding on to him as tight as she could. She wished she could freeze that moment in time and keep Kevin close to her forever. She knew she had to let go. Kevin loosened her grip from his shirt and held her out in front of him by her hands. Kelly began her nurturing spill.

"Call me every time you stop. I don't want to be here going crazy, wondering about you on the road. Definitely call me when you make it to your mom's. I wanna smell that serious Thanksgiving dinner I know she's cooking up."

Kevin laughed. "Girl, you crazy."

They both laughed and gave each other big bear hugs as they began walking outside to Kevin's car. They kissed, and Kelly stepped back on the sidewalk, trying to be brave, and waved goodbye.

"I'll call in about six or seven hours," Kevin hollered over the car as he folded himself into the driver's seat.

The tears began to roll again as Kelly waved and the love of her life drove off. Kelly didn't know why, and she tried to suppress the thoughts as much as possible. But she couldn't help but feel their relationship wouldn't survive this trial. She so desperately wanted to believe everything would be all right, so she continued about life as it would be, working hard in her classes and missing Kevin immensely.

Winter break was coming up soon, and everyone was making plans for the Christmas holiday. Kelly wasn't sure what she'd do with the extra time because she and Kevin usually visited both of their parents over the vacation and enjoyed the last two or three days together on the quiet campus, discovering more reasons and ways to love one another. Not this year.

Kevin had to work, possibly Christmas day and extra hours. Holidays were busy times at Mr. Rush's company. Good thing Kevin visited with his family for Thanksgiving because he wouldn't have any time to spend with anyone. He hated that he would not be able to see Kelly, but he was still staying with Mona's parents and saving his money to get a place and start his life as he envisioned it would be. It would be too much for him to send her a ticket and pay for a hotel, so he told her he would try to get off work for the New Year to come see her so they could spend time together like they usually do. That made Kelly happy, so she planned to go home for Christmas and return New Year's Eve to meet Kevin on Campus. She thought she might come back a day or so earlier just to make things perfect for their time together. To her, it had been too long since they've seen one another.

About a week before break, Kelly and some of her friends were having lunch at the student center. One of the girls in her group saw one of her friends and called her over.

"Hey, girl. How you doing?"

"Hey, Tracy. What's going on? I haven't seen you around lately."

"We've been here. It's you who've disappeared from general population." Tracy turned back to her group. "You guys remember Mona, don't you?"

They all agreed, grunted, and said hi and hello in unison.

"Hi, Mona!"

"Hey, Mona!"

"What's up, girl?"

"Hi." Kelly smiled as she spoke. She barely knew Mona, but she had seen her around campus and they shared a couple of the same friends.

"So what you doing for Christmas break?" Tracy asked Mona.

"I'm going home for the entire break to eat, shop, and be lazy."

Everyone chuckled a little in agreement with those plans.

"Yeah, and to sponge off your father, daddy's girl," Tracy teased Mona.

"Well, you know. 'Tis the season for giving, and I wouldn't want to damper Daddy's holidays by denying him the opportunity to give."

"Girl, you crazy," someone at the table teased.

"I just might do a little giving myself this year," Mona oozed out and cut her eyes toward Kelly. "Well, let me get out of here. Speaking of leaving, I have to get my tickets."

"All right, girl. Have fun. See you later," Tracy told Mona as she walked away toward the cashier.

"Bye," the rest of the table guest sang out.

Kelly looked at Tracy strangely with curiosity and asked her, "What are you doing for winter break, missy?" She knew how hard Tracy worked at that intern job because she wanted to get picked up permanently. "Don't tell me you're staying here working."

"Okay then, I won't tell you," Tracy said dryly. The rest of her friends were tuning up to get on her case. "Before y'all get started, you know the deal with me and this company, so don't even trip. I'll be off Christmas Day, so when I get off work Christmas Eve, I'm gonna drive up to Virginia and spend Christmas with my newly found aunt and get a good meal. All right?"

Just as quickly as the group tuned up, they shut up. They all knew Tracy was no-nonsense, and she was going to do what she had to do. Once her mind was made up, you were lucky if she even shared the information with you. They also knew she was right in her thinking, and sometimes you have to make sacrifices today to achieve tomorrow. Tracy wanted to stay in DC, her kindred hometown, and this architecture position would be just the thing to get her to her next level of plans.

Everyone understood Tracy and her plight, so they exchanged their well wishes and hugs when they finished lunch. They knew that would probably be the last time they saw each other before next year.

Kelly couldn't wait to see Kevin. She came home one day early to get prepared to have their very own Christmas and bring the New Year in right. She hadn't talked to Kevin since Christmas, but he told her he was sure he'd get New Year's Eve off or least get off early enough so he could catch a flight and get there before dark.

Kelly thought there would be a message on her machine from Kevin when she got back to her place, but he hadn't called yet. She couldn't call him because he was staying with his employers and did not want to abuse his welcome. He would call Kelly collect or on a phone card once or twice a week on his way home from work. Kelly didn't particularly like this arrangement, but she sort of understood his reasoning. Besides, he said he should have his own place within two months. She could live with that.

She cleaned her place immaculately. Although Kelly's place was always clean to the visiting eye, she was spring-cleaning in the dead of the winter. She didn't finish until almost one o'clock in the morning.

She was salty with sweat as she prepared for a nice, relaxing bath in her freshly cleaned tub. Kelly only thought about Kevin once while she was cleaning. She was glad she had plenty to do so she wouldn't be so impatient and worried. She figured he actually had to work and would be on the afternoon flight tomorrow and wanted to surprise her because he hadn't called with his flight number or anything for her to pick him up. For the rest of the night, she would do her hair, nails, and feet and pamper herself. Tomorrow, she would sleep late, then get up and go pick up some groceries for her menu that night and start cooking.

Kelly prepared flank steak and potatoes, a seafood casserole, cabbage, yams, and macaroni and cheese. She made a carrot cake for dessert. While she was preparing the last dish, she started getting a little worried and a tad bit irritated. She thought, *This better be a damn big surprise.*

After she put the casserole in the oven, she settled down to a cool, soothing bath. She decided to use each item in her gift set of Versace Crystal Noir. She knows how alluring that scent is and wanted to turn Kevin on to the nth degree. She figured he'd be sneaking in on her by the time she finished bathing or coming in shortly thereafter. Kelly bathed with the shower gel, smoothed the body lotion all over herself when she got out the tub, and finished up with the dusting powder. She bought a new negligee just for the night and slipped into it as she admired the perfectly matching polish of her manicure and pedicure. She even put a design on one of her toes and nails. She had to admit it, she looked good tonight.

"Who could resist this?" she said out loud, feeling kinda sexy. After she was completely satisfied with her reflection in the mirror, she put on the Chico DeBarge CD and tried not to notice it was almost nine o'clock. She propped herself up on the pillows in the bed and thumbed through catalogs. Now she was really getting angry.

*He really better have a good excuse for this. If he ain't hurt, I'm gonna kill him. He could have called and said something if his flight was delayed.* She knew the last flight went out at 5:10 p.m., and it was less than a four-hour trip. Kevin was supposed to be on the 3:00 p.m. flight, which is why Kelly was expecting him around seven-ish. *Here it is now, after ten o'clock and nothing. Didn't call to say dog, cat, fart, shit, or nothing.*

Kelly was through. This was beyond inconsiderate and completely unacceptable. She thought Kevin had been acting a little funny lately. The last time she talked to him on Christmas, he seemed a little preoccupied, but she figured it was because he was calling from the house where he was living with his boss's family. She thought maybe he was uncomfortable talking on their phone and didn't want to tie up their line.

*Something is up*, Kelly thought. *There I go again, being negative, thinking the worse.*

Kelly knew she would forget about every bad thought she just had if Kevin walked through that door, and she'd love him like she planned. She just wished that would actually happen because she was growing increasingly impatient and angry.

*That's it.* Kelly walked over and picked up the phone. She dialed the numbers so fast that she was surprised when the opposite line started ringing in her ear. She walked in circles, praying for someone to pick up.

"Hello?" a slightly groggy voice whispered.

"Tracy?" Kelly asked with relief that it was not the answering machine. "Girl, I didn't mean to wake you up. Why are you home? And asleep on New Year's Eve? Although I am glad you're home."

"Kelly? What's wrong girl?" She could hear the panic in Kelly's voice.

"If you don't mind, I'm gonna come over and tell you all about it when I get there."

"Of course, I don't mind. Come on. I'll come to life by the time you get here."

"Good. I'm bringing dinner. I'll be there ASAP, and we'll ring in the New Year together."

"Cool, I guess that beats my plans for ringing in the New Year, to just wake up and watch it slap me in the face, see if anything has changed. No resolutions, no expectations. That's not too exciting of a plan, is it?"

"No, missy, it's not, so here I come. See you in a bit."

Kelly hung up and started rushing around, packing up food and a bottle of wine. She got dressed quickly because she didn't want to be there if Mr. Kincaid decided to surface at the last hour. She also wanted to get to Tracy and tell her what happened in time enough to be good and drunk before the New Year arrived.

Tracy thought Kelly was going to knock her door down; she was banging on it so hard. Kelly had unloaded everything from the car and set it at Tracy's door by the time she started knocking.

"All right, I'm coming!" Tracy hollered as she walked to the door half-dressed. "You must be driving a rocket ship," she said as she opened the door, letting Kelly in. "I haven't even finished dressing, and you're already here, car unloaded, banging on the door, and staring at me with your pitiful party face on. I don't know if I should hug you or get a Band-Aid 'cause you look hurt."

"Do both. I'm ready to party, but I'm wounded," Kelly said with a half-smile.

Tracy hugged her friend and picked up some of the bags. Kelly grabbed the rest and followed her into the kitchen.

"You smell good, and you look good too. How come you aren't out partying?"

"Pour me a tall glass of wine and have a seat so I can pour out my lonely heart," Kelly told Tracy while she started preparing them a plate.

"What are you doing back here anyway?" Tracy asked.

"I came back yesterday because Kevin was supposed to meet me here, and we were going to spend New Year's Eve together," Kelly began explaining.

"Well, what happened?"

"I don't really know." *Gulp*. Kelly took one long swig of her wine. "He said he would try to get today off and come down last night, but if not, he'd come this afternoon."

"What did he say when you talked to him?" Tracy was trying to make sense of Kelly's story. She knew Kelly was emotional.

"I haven't talked to him since Christmas. I can't call him, and he hasn't called me."

"Wait, What! You can't call him? Why not?"

"He's living with the people he works for, and he doesn't want to disrespect their house…yada, yada, yada."

"Okay, and he hasn't called and said anything? Where was he coming from?"

"Michigan."

"Oh yeah, that's right. But that's weird. What kind of company does he work for where the owner lets the employee live with them?"

"Some construction company called Rush Enterprises." Tracy tensed a little as Kelly continued. "They are his friend's parents, and they let him stay for a while until he got settled. He said he'd be out of there in a couple of months, and everything would be cool."

Tracy got up and went into the kitchen while Kelly was talking. She came back with some cola and a bottle of Hennessy.

"The wine not enough, missy? I thought I was the one trying to drown my sorrows."

Tracy mixed them both a strong drink, and this time, Tracy took a big gulp. Her face became somber, and she looked straight into Kelly's face.

"That's Mona's last name," Tracy said in a loud whisper.

"What's Mona's last name? Mona who? What are you talking about, Tracy?"

"Rush, Mona Rush. She's from Michigan. That's her father's company where Kevin works. She said she was going home for the holidays to 'spend daddy's money.'"

Kelly looked at her perplexed. She didn't get it. She hated when Tracy would go off on a tangent and expect everyone to automatically clue in on what she was talking about.

"Just spit it out, Tracy. You're messing with my buzz here," Kelly said.

"Mona? In the student center?" Tracy said, rolling her hands in front of her, trying to help Kelly put the pieces of the puzzle together. She continued, "A couple of weeks ago, just before break? Mona Rush. She stopped at our table for a minute."

Kelly looked as if she was now following Tracy. She finally placed who the Mona was that Tracy was referring to in her mind. She still hadn't quite arrived at Tracy's location. Her expression indicated she wanted Tracy to make sense of why she brought up Mona's name.

"That's who Kevin is staying with—her parents. Mona's dad owns Rush Enterprises."

The connections nearly knocked Kelly off her seat. She inhaled her entire glass of Hennessy.

"That muthafucker! I don't believe he'd do something like that to me."

Tracy got scared. She was shocked. She'd never seen Kelly get this angry before. Kelly hardly ever cursed. She could tell Kelly wanted to tear up something, and she didn't want to be in the line of fire.

"He knew the whole time he wasn't coming here for New Year's Eve. He was just playing me like a fiddle. 'I don't wanna disrespect their house, my friend's dad, I'll call you.' Knowing all the time that I thought he was talking about a dude. Ain't that a bitch? 'Baby, I'll be there for New Year. I have to work on Christmas.' What kind of shit is that?" The more she thought about the things he had said, the angrier she got. "I knew a lot of that shit wasn't making sense, but I wanted to trust him. Why shouldn't I? I love him. I try to believe people until they give me a reason not to."

Tracy didn't know what to say. She felt like it was her fault Kelly was so upset. Why did she have to say anything? She told herself she should have waited until later to see what was really going on and approached it better. *Better? Who am I kidding? Kelly is my friend, and this news would have hurt her as much tomorrow as it does today. Besides, his ass should have been honest and up front with her. Why should I feel bad about him doing wrong? The only thing I feel bad about is Kelly's pain, but she would have hated me if she found out I knew and never said anything,* Tracy reasoned in her mind.

Tracy told Kelly, "Calm down. Let's think about this a little more. It doesn't have to be as bad as we're making it out to be."

Kelly broke down crying. She was hurt, mad, confused, and now, she was drunk. Her emotions were overflowing and out of control. She didn't know what she was feeling.

"It's not right. Whatever the situation is, it did not have to go down like this. He could have said something. If it's not bad as we're making it out to be, then what was he hiding? So it must be some dirt somewhere. If she's just a friend, why so secretive about the whole thing? I don't deserve this." She cried some more.

"Maybe they are just friends. He didn't know how you'd react, so he tried to keep everything quiet. You said he didn't plan to be there long. It could all be innocent," Tracy said, trying to get Kelly to think rationally. *Except for that Mona*, Tracy thought to herself.

"Well, why hasn't he called? Just leave me hanging like this? Like some kind of trick on the street? And why isn't he here, Tracy?" Kelly demanded.

Tracy couldn't answer any of those questions. Kelly was no airhead. You couldn't tell her just any old thing. And she certainly was too smart to allow herself to be mistreated. She really loved Kevin. That's why she chose to believe what he told her. But she was no one's fool.

Kevin couldn't bring himself to call Kelly New Year's Day. He didn't have anything to say for himself. He knew the longer it took to call, the worse things would get. He also knew it probably couldn't get any worse. If Kelly found out, she would leave him for sure, but isn't that what he wanted—freedom and space? No, not this way. He never planned for anything to go down like this. How could he be so weak? He wanted to enjoy his life, get on the path of the future he envisioned for himself, and not get caught up in a web with someone who runs in the same circle as his girl. Not his boss's daughter. If he hurts her feelings, he might as well kiss his job goodbye. Man, none of this was part of the plans. He was doomed from the start.

Kevin reviewed the situation in his head and fussed at himself. *I should have known nothing would come that easily. She was just too friendly, too helpful. She was up to something. She wasn't even supposed to come out here for the holidays, so she said. Right! The fellas was right. 'You can't trust 'em, man. Trying to be friends with the opposite sex is like a man having a baby. It ain't gonna happen'. Now what am I gonna do? I should have paid closer attention to the warning signs. She called home rather frequently and always asked to speak to me. Then her holiday travel plans changed. After taking up all my free time hanging out, dinner and movies as friends, she slips her ass in my room.*

*She had the whole thing planned. I got played. I noticed after I mentioned I was going to see Kelly for the New Year, she started clinging to me, and suddenly, I had to work New Year's Eve. Then the night before New Year's Eve, I come in late and tired, and the house is empty. I go straight to bed because I'm exhausted from trying to finish up as much work as possible in order to leave early the next day. She eases into my room, and when I wake up, she's all over me. I was weak. Damn it, I fell for it. Now I'm sitting here all fucked up and confused about my future when I thought I had it all together. I really don't want to lose Kelly under these circumstances. Maybe it won't get that bad. Maybe she won't find out. Maybe Mona feels just as bad as I do and will never mention it again. And maybe pigs fly! Why am I sitting here tripping? How come I can't get up the nerves to call her? No one knows anything yet. Man, I'm really tripping.*

Mona couldn't wait to get back to class after winter break. She chose her bait carefully. She told Ceree all about her trip and, most importantly, about her night with Kevin when *he* seduced her. Oh, but she wasn't mad. "He's so tender and a real great lover." She knew Ceree couldn't hold water and would tell Tracy, who would be sure to tell Kelly. She would leave him, and he was sure to be all hers.

Mona's plan worked like a charm. Everything got back to Kelly in less than twenty-four hours. By the time Kevin was feeling a little less guilty and thought he wouldn't give off any signs of a problem or guilt, he called Kelly. After all the time passing and standing Kelly up, he called one Thursday after work like everything was normal. It might have been normal for him, but Kelly made some changes. Kelly's number was disconnected, just like her relationship with Kevin. Kelly didn't play that; she had her number changed to an unlisted one the same day she got the news. She was through being naïve and understanding. Everyone has choices, and apparently, she was not his.

"Well, if that's what you want Kevin, you got it," Kelly fussed out loud by herself. She tried to figure out what she would do. "You're a lot of man but not enough for two. Uh-uh, that will never do. It was all so tacky that you can never come back. I can't be with someone that stupid and weak. Why couldn't he just break it off first? Why did it have to be someone I know? Whatever. Peace, my brother!"

Kelly was sick. Her heart was broken; torn in two. She didn't know what she would do, but she knew what she wouldn't do. She would not be caught up in any drama, and as long as Mona didn't flex on her, she wasn't tripping. Kelly had goals. She couldn't let anything or anyone stop her from achieving her success. She dove deeper into her books, made contacts on the West Coast, and submitted resumes to every company that met her salary and career goals. She even applied to a few that didn't, just in case. But she wasn't too worried about getting what she wanted. She still had job offers that stood from undergraduate school.

Every day, it hurt a little less, and by the time graduation came, Kelly was full of her future. She glowed with all the opportunities that lay ahead for her.

# Josh

"DARK GABLE," MAX ANNOUNCED. "WHAT'S going on?"

Everyone turned to see Josh as he entered the room. Josh was so masculine and fine that they named him the black Clark Gable.

"Still up to your old tricks, huh, Max?" Josh teased.

"Man, if you weren't my brother, I'd take you and handcuff you and..." Max flirted.

"Girl, I ain't your brother, and you wouldn't do nothing with your pseudo married ass," Josh chastised.

Chan offered her availability. "I ain't your sister, I ain't married, I ain't scared, and I got some handcuffs." She pulled out her cuffs and dangled them in the air.

The rest of the ladies hollered and gave each other high fives as Josh tried not to be embarrassed. He was used to their teasing, but he could not believe Chan broke out with some cuffs.

"Girl, you better put those things up before the locals call management or the police on you."

"I am the police, and what? Are you scared?" Chan asked.

"Here you go." Josh blew Chan's remark off.

"I'm just kidding." Chan got up to hug and kiss Josh on the cheek. "But you know you're hella fine, and our day wouldn't go right if we didn't mess with you. Especially since we can't have you."

"Well, that was y'all call. All your rules and boundaries. Want to keep everything all platonic and stuff. Cause otherwise, I'd take all four of you, at once." He paused, pulling on his waistband, flexing his masculinity. "Right here, Right now. Spread your butts across the buffet table." Josh laughed and took his seat. "You guys the ones always taken, tied up with some weak brotha. When a real brother come your way, you wanna treat him like your baby brother. It's cool though. I still love you guys. I'll be your *big* brother." Josh leaned in, looked over toward Kelly, and got a little serious. "Except you, girl. You know I been after you since we met. I'm not going out like that with that brother crap. After all these years, you still not gonna give a brother some play? What's up with that, Kelly?"

"So how's your girl, Josh?" Kelly asked.

Deflated, Josh answered, "She's fine." He sat back in his chair. "Thanks for asking."

"So when are you going to let us meet her, Josh?" Dede asked.

"Let it go, Dede. I got some rules of my own. Y'all know none of my girlfriends get in this circle. Not so you bigmouth femme fatales can get a hold of her, pollute her mind. and get all up in my business. Not as long as I still think I got a chance with Miss Kelly here." He smirked at Kelly and caressed her hand.

"Josh, please." Kelly took her hand away and tapped him playfully across his forearm.

"Josh, how's your mom doing?" Max asked.

"She's good. Missing you guys. She said she is going to have to fix a peach cobbler to get her girls to come by," Josh told them.

"Now she know she knows how to get our attention. Visiting your mom has never been a problem. Give the date and time, and we're there," Chan chimed in. "Max, you should be ashamed of yourself staying away from Mrs. Dawson for so long."

"Me? I didn't want to wear out my welcome. We were just at her table three weeks ago," Max defended herself.

"Now you all know if you came by every day, it still wouldn't be enough for her. Especially since my sister is gone."

"That's right. How's she doing anyway?" Chan asked.

"She's fine. She's thinking about studying abroad next semester for her junior year."

"That's cool. Tell her we said hi and good luck."

"I already did," Josh responded.

"So, Josh, you really like this girl you're seeing now? Hear you pretty serious with this one," Dede asked.

"Yeah, she's cool. We've been hanging out quite a bit lately. She's pretty fun. Decent sense of humor, good job, and has a life of her own. If only she could cook, I'd ask her to marry me today."

"Sure. You men always have an excuse not to get married," Chan said.

"I'm a growing boy, got to get my eat on, and besides, it would destroy any marriage if the husband was running over to his mom's house four or five times a week. I must have good home-cooked meals," Josh told them.

"Your species always has some prerequisite. Why can't you just take women as they are?" Dede jumped in.

"It's a prerequisite, a pro-requisite, a corequisite, and any other requisite you can think of. Basically, it's a solo requisite. She can be fat, skinny, fucked-up weave, bald, and toothless, but if she can whip up some tasty-ass vittles, I'm home every night."

"What about intimacy and a family?" Dede inquired.

"I got that covered. Unlike good cooking, sex comes a dime a dozen. Her job is to cook so good that I want to make love to her, and I'll make love to her so good that she'll want to cook. We'd be a tag team. Together forever, eating and making love. No babies though. It's a breeding thang. If she's a monster, can't go around bringing more monsters in the world," Josh answered.

"I swear you're stupid," Max laughed.

"What?" Josh tried to be oblivious to his humor. "Man, I'm telling you. Feed a brother, and he will call again. That's why all of you sitting around here entertaining each other. All that new millennium shit. I got…I want…I'm doing…I don't need…And ain't got no man! Why? Cause you can't cook. Or won't cook. Think I'm lying? Leave a message with one of those brothers you talking to and tell him you're cooking a serious meal. I bet he'll be there, without calling back, on time, bottle of wine in hand. And you don't even tell him it was for him! Just mention cooking, and now he got time. I'm serious. Try it, so y'all can get a man of your own and stop giving me so much grief. Except you Kelly." Josh winked at Kelly and pursed his lips flirtatiously.

"Shut up, Josh," Dede joked. "Just because you're all that don't mean you have all the answers and everyone is jocking you."

"Now, Dede, you know you jocking anything in a pair of slacks!" Joshed teased her back.

Everyone laughed. They knew Dede was a little loose, and if Josh let her, she'd be all over him. Since she wasn't getting any play, she accepted their friendship and loved Josh like she loved the rest of her friends.

"Well, that may be true but not you," Dede confessed teasingly.

"I'm gonna start round two. This shrimp linguini is jamming." Josh headed back to the buffet table.

"Yeah, you do need a wife who can cook. The way you eat, you'd go broke eating out, trying to feed yourself," Max said as she got up to follow.

"I don't see you missing any meals, ma'am," Josh shot back.

"You know I'm a growing girl," Max teased.

"Mm-hm, and in all the right places. You just 'grow' ahead," Josh joked.

"Careful now. You know I got a jealous husband," Max playfully warned.

The rest of the members at the table laughed and got up to head to the dessert table. Dede's plate had a pile of sweets on it. She enjoyed eating and had no shame in displaying her pleasure.

"Dang, Dede, you think you have enough?" Chan observed.

"Shut up, Chan. You're just jealous," Dede said.

"You know what? You're right! In fact, I hate you. You always pig out, and look at you—slim and trim," Chan responded.

"She needs to take that cake and stick it to her hips. Put a little fat on those bones," Josh picked with Dede.

"Forget you, Josh, but if I could, I would slap a cupcake or two up here," Dede said, cupping her breast.

"I should have that problem. If I just look at sweets too long, my ass swells. *Paiyow!*" Kelly slapped her hip.

"Girl, don't you change a thang. I like that little trailer you got hitched to the back of you. A brother can sit his drink on it. A skinny woman can't do nothing for me except point which way the juicy woman went," Josh interjected, addressing Kelly.

"I happen to like my slender physique. Everybody ain't supposed to be big-boned or voluptuous," Dede defended herself.

"Yeah, but sistahs ain't supposed to be anorexic or flat as a board either. One curve or detour on the road makes for an interesting drive, you know what I mean? I'm just kidding, Dede. You know you're fly with your sexy, little model figure. You ladies know you actually represent the beauty of a black woman. All shapes, shades, and sizes, and *fine* in your own right."

"Yeah, yeah, try and clean it up," Dede said sarcastically.

"Seriously, all of you are fine. Why do you think I hang around you? You all are good for a brother's rep."

"All right, you guys. Let's go before Josh puts the buffet out of business," Kelly said.

Kelly stood up and started gathering her things and digging in her purse for her share of the tip. They always tipped well. None of them were stingy customers to waiters, so when they were together, that waiter usually got a real treat—at least three dollars from each of them. Since this place was buffet, the bus person got big bucks for very little work.

Josh got up and sat his five bucks on top of Kelly's money. "Yeah, I better run. Not all of us are corporate executives and can lunch all day."

"But I can always bank on you keeping me grounded with your cynicism and all," Kelly responded.

"Look who's talking Mr. Investment Banker who's never at his desk," Max teased.

"Except all that time is usually spent with clients, not having fun. Although I do enjoy my job," Josh stated.

"I know you're not insinuating I don't work hard. Man, let me tell you something…" Kelly started in on Josh.

"Here ya'll go again. You fuss like an old married couple. Josh, why you always do that to Kelly?" Chan asked.

"Cause she's so sexy when she gets riled up. She know I'm just playing with her. I just like to see her excited. You know I love a woman with some spunk in her," Josh said.

"Both of you need to quit. Just go ahead and do the nasty and get that anxiety between the two of you out," Dede suggested.

The rest of the group laughed, and Kelly began her bye-byes. She hugged everyone and told them she'd talk to them later. Max hugged everybody and kissed Josh on the cheek. Josh passed out his big bear hugs and kissed everyone goodbye.

"I'll see you guys at church Sunday," Josh said.

"Come here. Let me kiss that bald chocolate head of yours, you hunk of a man you," Chan told Josh.

"Okay, see everyone Sunday. What service?" Dede asked.

"Early morning, eight o'clock, of course. It's football season. Josh ain't missing no games. He got a deal with the man upstairs," Kelly teased.

"All right, everybody. See you later." Chan walked away first.

"Bye-bye."

"See you Sunday."

"Love you, guys."

"*Au revoir.*"

"Okay, folks. Bye now." Max closed out the chant and headed for her car.

When Josh got back to work, there were several messages waiting for him. His clients were always calling him, checking on the latest changes in their investment package. He wondered if they ever stopped to think about when he'd have time to actually work on their files since they were so regularly taking up his time on the phone. Josh finds time—in fact, he makes time—to give special attention to all his clients and their portfolios. He works long, hard hours and has a home office where he works equally as diligently. Josh has made money for the novice middle-income investor to the million-dollar high-risk investors. Many of his clients are athletes and in the entertainment industry. His popularity came by word of mouth and referrals. The strength in his professional career lies in the equal treatment he gives to all his clients. His biggest reward and praises come from the joy his average-income clients' exhibit when he reports earnings on their investment. He is fully aware of the difficulty of separating from your savings and having no other means of replacing that money.

The fear and anxiety his new clients experience when they make a decision to attempt investing has a lasting impression on Josh. For those reasons, he strives for high numbers on their rate of return and tries to keep their risk as minimal as possible.

Josh remembers the time Mr. Jessip kept him on the phone for almost an hour, inquiring about his funds. Mr. Jessip only started the portfolio with about seven thousand dollars, but that seven thousand dollars did not come easy for him. He wanted to be sure his money was doing all right and he had not gotten scammed. He felt pretty comfortable with Josh, but he still couldn't sit idly by and watch his money disappear. He wanted to understand all the tricks his dollars were doing and just maybe he'd add to the package after he saved some more. He certainly had plenty questions for Josh and was enthusiastic about learning as much as he could digest about investing.

"Mr. Jessip, your stock is doing fine. In fact, since the last quarter, your stock has almost doubled," Josh explained.

"Oh, good. It doubled. How can I track the activity on my stock if I want to know what it's doing day to day?" the voice on the other end of the phone asked.

"Just dial that number listed in the package I gave you when you opened the account, and it will give you the balance and current changes in the market. But I wouldn't advise calling daily, Mr. Jessip. The market fluctuates so regularly that you'd make yourself sick watching those single points rise and fall. Try to be patient and not think about it so much. I know that will be hard to do, but it will get easier as time passes," Josh advised.

"What about this market fall I've been hearing about? I listen for that stuff on the news now. It seems like every day, they're saying the economy is getting worse, and investors are losing. Should I take my money out?" the concerned voice inquired.

"No, not at all, Mr. Jessip. I invested your money in some real conservative stock. The market isn't crashing. It fluctuates like that all the time. Now wouldn't be a good time to sell because you would lose money that you've earned. It's a good time to buy on certain stock, and that's what I'll be looking into to further divest your package. Let it sit there and earn, and when it's time, we'll sell high."

"I know it may not be much to you, but that seven thousand dollars made us miss some meals or clothing or needed car repairs. It didn't come easy," Mr. Jessip confided.

"I understand, Mr. Jessip, believe me I do. I've missed my share of meals and shopping sprees too. How about we do this? When the stock earns enough to have other money working for it, I'll transfer that initial investment to an interest-earning fund. That way, your money is secure, and the new money can work for you without you feeling like you're gambling," Josh suggested.

"You can do that?" Mr. Jessip perked up. "That would help me relax. I sure appreciate your help, Mr. Dawson."

"Not a problem. My job is to help you. I appreciate you giving me the opportunity to make your money perform and trusting me to do it," Josh said graciously.

"Sir, you are a gem. I'll talk to you next week," Mr. Jessip said before hanging up.

Josh laughed. Mr. Jessip would certainly be calling him next week, if not sooner. He knew even once he transferred the funds to a savings package, Mr. Jessip would worry about the new money and its performance. Josh didn't mind. Like the other clients, he would eventually learn to rest easier about the market, and the calls and stress would lessen.

As much as Josh loves his job, it was increasingly becoming a burden to be in the office daily. His female supervisor was regularly and blatantly expressing her interest in Josh, and he's afraid rejecting her could have severe repercussions. Not only did Josh avoid comingling with Janessa because they worked together, he also thought she was butt ugly. Very smart, knew her job, deserved her position, but she was hard to look at. Uglier than sin warmed over twice. The foundation of her ugly wasn't necessarily from birth. It was greatly contributed to attitude and the tendency to do too much for improvement. She wears really big, really bad hair.

With as much money as she makes, she has this low-budget OW (obvious weave) that isn't maintained very well. It has several colors streaked through, and her actual hair is kinky at the roots and over-permed on the ends with super straight hair sewn in that is tangled and matted toward the bottom. It also extends to the middle of her back. Her acrylic fingernails seem about three inches long and are always painted in some gaudy, flashy colors. As if the fingernails weren't bad enough, she has long acrylic toe nails that are usually painted identical to the fingernails. Her makeup is almost indescribable or, at best, should not be described or duplicated. The foundation is obvious tones off from her actual complexion. It appears she uses a beige 2 when she is clearly a mocha 3. Her blush and eye shadow appear to come from the same lipstick tube. And the lips, oh boy. They are heavily outlined with a black eyeliner pencil and filled in with a bright magenta that is usually smeared all over her face by ten o'clock in the morning. Every couple of weeks, she gets these long eyelashes put on that could cause a global freeze if she batted her eyes too rapidly. By the end of that week, the lashes are lifting off her eyelid and falling down her face.

Although her legs are big and shapely, her style of dress is usually unprofessional and not becoming of an executive or any person in a position to set examples. Her skirts and dresses are generally quite short and quite tight. The large waistline does not add to the beauty of her outfits. The employees wonder what in the heck she does with her money. It's obvious it isn't used toward good grooming and a skilled stylist. One of the other female investment officers keeps reminding them you can't always teach class and style. She believes her supervisor's money is wasted on junk purchases.

"When you buy poor quality and take bad care of it, you end up buying over and over again. Although there is one visible and quality purchase she made—that funky, funky ass Porsche. It is bad. She also has a pretty decent house in the hills in a predominantly white neighborhood. Her subordinates wonder what those white folks must make of Janessa. According to her, they love her, and they probably do. You know white folks always intrigued by the oddity and activity of black folk. Any opportunity to be in black folks' business and qualify their views of them, they love 'em or hate 'em. Depending on whether they feel threatened by them or not."

She doesn't even have a clue about how others see her. Not that one should be overly concerned with others' view of them, but good Lord, eccentricity and anything else in excess can become negative. Janessa knew how to make money earn money, and she had plenty of toys to prove it. They were appealing to the average individual, and this was her usual method of attracting her mates. Many guys used her for her material things. Janessa was subconsciously aware of it but chose to ignore the obvious and tell herself they would stay.

Josh was neither impressed nor interested in Janessa or her toys. He did feel bad for her and the many terrible relationships she encountered. Janessa really wasn't a bad person but just not for Josh. Since some of her relationships got really ugly when they broke off, Josh wasn't sure what to expect of Janessa if he rejected her flatly, so he measured his recourse.

Janessa must have sensed Josh was avoiding her and ignoring her advances because she had been acting a little flaky lately. She'd been giving him grief over small, insignificant matters. As much time as the investment officers spent in the field, she was starting to monitor his field time more closely and regularly. She was taking issue with his phone calls, questioning if they were business or personal. Her charades were starting to get to Josh.

Josh had an appointment with a client who was well-dressed and beautiful. Janessa assumed she was a personal friend due to their personable and friendly communication. Janessa walked into Josh's office making requests for very nonurgent information and with attitude.

"Oh, I see you have company," Janessa stated, looking down at the client in Josh's office.

"Carol, this is Janessa, my supervisor. Actually, she just arrived. We haven't quite got started. Is there something I can help you with?" Josh asked.

"I need to know the status on the Kasner file and what you plan to do with the F fund," Janessa said.

"The stats are in the current report I gave you earlier this week. I can't make any changes to their F funds until the projections come out. You know those won't be available for at least three weeks," Josh responded, puzzled that Janessa was inquiring about the Kasner file.

"Well, I need a full report on their current standings, next quarter's estimated returns, the three-year comparisons, and how you plan to divide their funds to attract better earnings for the upcoming year," Janessa demanded.

Josh sensed it wasn't necessarily the Kasner portfolio that interested Janessa, but something else was bothering her. He couldn't quite put his finger on what it could be, but he knew he had to diffuse the current situation. He would try later to get an understanding of what was going on with Janessa. Maybe it was one of those boyfriends again.

"Okay, I'll get on it right away. I'll have it on your desk at the end of the week," Josh said patiently.

"Try tomorrow," Janessa said sharply. She walked out the office and left the door open.

"Nice boss," Carol said laughingly as she got up to close the door.

Josh apologized for Janessa's behavior, giving the excuse of tension in their business due to the recent market drops and loss of one of their major shareholders to a larger firm in New York.

"She's actually not that bad. There's been a lot of pressure on management to jump-start the market, satisfy shareholders, and attract new investors," Josh explained.

"You know, you're really something. She storms in here attacking your professional aptitude and flexing her supervisory muscles, and you still defend her. Moreover, she does something so stupid as talking about other clients' business in front of the competition and reveals the incompetence of the investment officer in front of the customer," Carol summarized.

"Hey, who you calling incompetent?" Josh interjected.

"You know what I mean. That's how others would interpret it. Luckily, I'm fully aware of your capabilities and strengths in this money-making field. Anyone else would have walked out, and this firm would have one less client. The most amazing part is she did all this with no regard to the 'company' sitting in your office. Or should I say, blatant disregard for present 'company'? She was so full of emotion. Did you see how she looked at me? I think she likes you," Carol laughed at her revelation.

Josh laughed, trying to suppress his discomfort. He was surprised at the accuracy of Carol's observation. He only hoped Janessa's attraction to him was not that obvious to everyone. He couldn't believe she had taken it this far. He had to do something about this before it got further out of hand. Immediately.

"If only she did, life around here would be much easier. I don't think she likes anyone," Josh joked, trying to deflect the clients revelation and ease the pressure he was feeling to keep this whole incident professional. "Well, we better get started. I'm sure you're anxious to get the numbers and performance appraisals for this quarter."

"Yes, I would like to see those items, but I'm here for a totally different reason," Carol stated with a serious tone.

Josh straightened up in his chair. He looked at Carol with intense concern. He hoped she wasn't there to close their account. He always made money for their company. He knew the market was on the downslope right now, but that was how stocks worked. It wasn't nearly as bad as it was in 2008 when they lost all those millions of dollars. He thought if ever there was a time he'd lose them as clients, it would have been then. Now the money was steady. No major earnings, but Josh divided the money in safe markets to prevent loss. He thought, at worst, they were content with his work. How could he have been so far off base in knowing his clients and their expectations? Josh braced himself for the next release of syllables from Carol's mouth.

"Our parent company, Desitaur Manufacturing, did an in-house audit of our books for the past three years. They asked how long we've been connected with your investment firm and requested statistics and appraisals over the last five to seven years. To make a short story long, when they completed the audit, they decided to let you handle our southeastern region of their investment portfolio. They placed me in charge of deciding which companies and how much budget for which to allow you to create packages and monitoring the activity you set them up with. Josh, I know your work, and I personally have no worries that you will make sensible, aggressive, and profitable decisions. I will try not to make a pest of myself with phone calls and visits, but you will hear from me a little more often than in the past. I have a vested interest in the success of these investments, and the GMs will expect regular reports on the performance of their stocks until they see steady growth and can relax about this new decision."

Josh let out a sigh of relief. "I fully understand. I'll do some research this weekend, get some numbers together, and send you a proposal on how we will handle the investment and the probable returns. How does a three-year projections sound?" Josh jumped on the offer.

"Excellent, Josh. I feel good about this already. I knew you were the one to come to with this offer. Josh, you've got yourself a billion-dollar contract. Here's the reports of our earnings over the past three years and next year's projected earnings. Also, the reviews, earnings, and divisions of our portfolio with our current investment firm. Now make us some money and yourself a little bit while you're at it." Carol smiled as she pushed the files over to Josh and stood up to leave.

Josh stood and shook Carol's hand. "Thanks, Carol. I appreciate your trust. I won't let you down."

"My pleasure, Josh. This isn't blind faith. You've proved yourself capable time and time again. You be sure to tell captain manager that if I had been a new client, she would have blown a billion-dollar opportunity for her company. I'll look for that report in the next week or so and set up an appointment with the executives early the following week."

"Okay, see you then. I'll be ready."

Josh walked Carol to their floor lobby, made certain her valet parking ticket was validated, and shook her hand again. Josh marched back to his office and retrieved his copy of the current statistic report of the Kasner portfolio from his files. He grabbed the reports Carol left him and headed to Janessa's office.

"Here's the copy of the Kasner report. And, Janessa, that was Carol, the CEO of accounting for Alias Industries. These are copies of their financial standings and investments and stock activity for the past three years. They want us to handle a billion-dollar portfolio for the southeastern region of their parent company. Luckily, we have a decent track record with them and she has some faith in our work because she was not impressed with your unprofessional intrusion on our meeting." Josh turned to walk out the office.

Janessa was stunned and embarrassed. She knew the Alias account holders preferred to meet with Josh when making inquiries or changes to their account. She'd never met Carol and didn't stop to think when he introduced her that she could be the Carol of Alias Industries. When she saw those great pair of legs walk by Josh's assistant and the warmth with which he greeted her, jealousy overrode her ability to think rationally. Janessa couldn't believe she had gotten this far out of control. This schoolgirl crush was becoming a bit much. Had she blown that account, the company would have axed her without second thought. She knew she truly owed Josh an apology. He could have easily gone to the executives and told them what happened. Even though the account is still available, they probably would have fired her anyway or taken away her major accounts and investment officers. The loss of her top investment consultants, which includes Josh, would result in a decrease in her performance ratings and ultimately lead to her dismissal. Actually, Janessa thought she'd probably lose Josh anyway. This account is sure to get him a promotion. They'll be on equal playing fields at that point.

"Josh," Janessa called out. Josh stopped and turned to see what she wanted. "I found my copy of the Kasner report. Josh, I sincerely apologize for my behavior in your office earlier," Janessa said. Her voice begged for forgiveness. "It was unprofessional and unwarranted. It won't happen again. There was no reason for me to attack your work standard and performance. Again, I apologize for my actions today and my inexcusable acts over the past several weeks. Also, disregard that report I requested for tomorrow." She handed Josh the Alias reports back. "Focus your attention on preparing this proposal. Schedule an appointment with me for Monday or Tuesday, and we can review the report and some strategies to make their money multiply. I'll schedule a meeting with the board to inform them on the particulars of our new client and to get approval of the final draft for presentation to the Alias parent company executives."

Josh took the folders. "I'm on it. I'll probably need you late into Monday evening so we can sharpen up the figures and brainstorm on the expectations and responses of the board," Josh said with enthusiasm as he headed out the door. He hoped Janessa would adhere to her decision, and there would be no further conflict between them. He didn't harp on what happened. He figured she was embarrassed enough, and he just wanted to forget the whole ordeal.

"I'll clear my calendar!" Janessa yelled after him. "And, Josh, thanks."

Josh looked back with understanding. "You're welcome."

Josh went to his office and prepared an outline for the Alias account. He tied up loose ends on other files and spent the rest of the week dividing stock and funds in the portfolios of his current investors.

Josh pulled up to his condo and unloaded a crate of files, reports, and stock analysis. He prepared himself mentally to be submerged in files and saturated with numbers all weekend. Once he got all his belongings inside, Josh ordered Chinese food and activated his "all work and no play" mode. He put on his old college athletic sweats. The bottoms were all torn up and worn out. There was a hole in the lower right butt cheek that came from sliding to bases when he played softball. The waistband was shredded from wash and wear and tear. The string barely had any material to hold onto to keep his pants up. His mother and sister hated those sweats. Josh would put them on no sooner than company would visit and come downstairs talking and smiling with everyone like he had on a three-piece tux. They threw them away on a couple of occasions, and Josh would throw a royal fit. He'd retrieve them and tell them those were his performance pants. They helped him relax, focus, and think more competitively. They couldn't argue the relax factor. How could anyone not be comfortable in those things? It was almost like wearing nothing.

Josh had a basic routine for long work weekends. He would rent several movies, order takeout all weekend, and not answer the phone. He would not come out the house except maybe to empty out the trash if the takeout odors got too unbearable. After working on his project for several hours, he'd take a meal break and watch some of his movies, or he'd fall asleep for thirty or forty-five minutes if he was tired. He'd have a marathon-type work weekend where he'd work, eat, and nap for about seventy-two hours.

Sometimes one of the girls or all the girls would stop by on GP. They were used to Josh when he was in this mode. They usually didn't bother him much when they'd catch him this way. On an occasion or two, they would take over the TV or movies and food. They still stayed out of his way but would watch his movie and eat up the day's order of takeout. They would order or pick up some more food for him after they were through invading his world.

Josh didn't mind their visits. They knew how to give him his space, and when he was really focused, he'd forget they were there anyway. And sometimes he needed that additional sense of life around him. Otherwise, he'd get so engrossed with work that it would seem like the rest of the world vanished, so he appreciated their presence. In addition, if he had to bounce some ideas around, he'd have someone else to talk to other than himself. The times when no one came by and he stayed secluded or sequestered for all those days were the most difficult. Not so much while he was working but when he finished and realized he'd been out of touch for so long. It made him appreciate the hustle and bustle of the city, friends, family, and human contact.

When Josh completed his project, he'd clean his place, clean himself, and get out his condo to do something, anything, that involved people. He had to reconnect to life. Josh couldn't imagine how agonizing it must feel to be in a depressed state. To lose the desire to see or talk to someone or come out the house or bedroom. Unable to smile or share your purpose or gift in life. These moments made him better understand the suicidal thoughts involving depression. He felt like such an existence would make life unbearable and eventually have you utterly insane.

Josh was taking a meal and movie break when his doorbell chimed. It was his girlfriend, Carla. She came over because Josh had not come by to pick her up, and she kept getting the answering service when she called. Josh walked over to the door and looked through the peephole. He opened the door.

"Hey, baby," Josh said, a little surprised to see her. Josh leaned to kiss her as she walked in.

Carla walked right passed Josh, missing his kiss. "What happened to you, Josh?" she asked.

"Oh, this is just my thinking clothes. I wear this when I have a lot of work—" Josh was chuckling about her inquiry of his outfit.

"No," Carla cut him off. "What happened to you picking me up this evening? We were supposed to go to dinner and to the musical."

"Oh damn! I completely forgot. I had this big account come up, and I had to get this report ready by Monday," Josh said apologetically, trying to explain his situation.

"So you just didn't call or anything?" Carla was getting angrier.

"I'm sorry, babe. Let me make it up to you. We'll go next weekend," Josh said.

"The show ends this weekend. Josh, why didn't you call and say something? You don't look that busy to me, sitting around eating and watching movies. Were you gonna ignore me all weekend and act like nothing happened? When were you gonna say something, Josh? I'm not worth a courtesy phone call to you? What kind of way is that to treat someone you supposedly care about?" Carla quizzed.

"Look, girl, I said I completely forgot. Not on purpose. I wasn't ignoring you. If the thought escaped me, how can I intentionally do you wrong? Something really important came up at work. It took over all my thoughts and free time, and it's going to consume my entire weekend."

"So this something is more important to you than me and the two of us spending time together? I haven't seen you or talked to you all week. What kind of way is that for a couple to act?" Carla asked, still angry.

"Ah, come on now. Don't start with that foolishness. You know my work is important to me. Sometimes things like this will happen. The show is going to Savannah next week. We can spend the weekend up there," Josh said, getting a little bit irritated with her last statement.

"Oh, so I'm just supposed to wait for you and whenever you're ready for us to get together? Never mind any plans," Carla spewed.

"You know what? This isn't getting anywhere. We missed the show, I apologized, and I can't unscramble those eggs. If you just want to argue, you'll have to do that by yourself. I have a lot of work to do. That is all I'm doing this weekend. You heard my offer. Take it or leave it. You decide what you wanna do."

"I'll leave it. You're insensitive and selfish. You don't want a real relationship. You want to do what you want to do, when you want to do it. It's not only about you. You need to consider others and how your actions affect them. Since you wanna act like you're the only one who matters, then be with your damn self." Carla stormed out of Josh's place.

Josh looked at the door she had just walked through with disbelief. *Damn, all that? I simply forgot. It's not like I've done this to her before. I said I'd make it up to her. Man, was that extreme or what? Was all that necessary? Imagine if I really did something serious, like miss her birthday or date her friend or something?* Josh thought to himself. "She would have me executed. Oh well, if her understanding is that bad this early in the relationship, it's best she's gone. She'll end up being some kind of fatal attraction or something. She couldn't cook anyway!" Josh said out loud.

Josh decided not to spend any time trying to figure out that dramatic scene. He had plenty enough work to keep him occupied. He was already focused on numbers and market matching. He would simply jot that little episode on a Post-it and stick it away.

He sat back down to finish his food and watch some of the movie. He was watching *Reservoir Dogs*, and before the weekend was up, he would see *Friday*, his all-time favorite, and *Bourne Identity*.

Josh liked having Chinese food on the first night of his shut-in because it didn't overfill him and make him sluggish. He generally worked more diligently on Friday evenings than the other nights. He finished his first round of chow and watched about ten more minutes of the movie. He got up, went to the bathroom, came back, and dove right back into his work.

When Josh looked up from the computer and the papers and reports spread over his desk, it was almost two o'clock in the morning. Josh didn't think he was tired, but he could sure use something to eat. He grabbed some more food and sat in front of the TV.

He was about three quarters of the way through the movie when he finished eating. He figured he would go ahead and watch the rest of that one, work about two more hours, and start a new movie tomorrow afternoon. Or should he say today afternoon.

Not ten minutes had passed before Josh was out cold. The movie played to the end and stopped itself. Josh woke up at about five in the morning, mad at himself.

"Damn, I'm just now supposed to be going to sleep, and here I am waking up. I didn't finish watching the movie or choosing the investment divisions for the financial package. That knocks me off schedule. All right, I gotta correct that now. I'll eat breakfast and finish this movie," Josh scolded and gathered himself.

Josh rewound the movie to what he last remembered seeing. He fixed himself a large bowl of cereal and sat down to eat and watch the last bit of *Reservoir Dogs*.

Now Josh was ready. He was refreshed. He had himself a decent light breakfast and a really good nap. He would be able to work for hours.

By the time Josh finished Sunday evening, he had missed church and all the football games. He knew better than to turn on the TV to try and watch the games for any period of time. He would have ended up coaching, catching, running, hollering, and cheering with the players until the very last play of the last game and not have done an ounce of work. He would have to settle for the highlight tapes during the sports reviews. But right now, he had to get out of the house or get someone in it. He needed some signs of life. He opened all the windows, straightened the clutter at his desk, picked up all the trash and took it outdoors, cleaned the house, and changed the sheets on his bed.

Josh left quickly and got in his car and started driving as he decided who he'd call or go see. He welcomed the sound of traffic and the stars that were blooming above. He drove by one of his buddies, but no one was there. He decided to call Max. He knew he would get grief for missing church that morning. At least until he got a chance to tell them what was going on this weekend. He hadn't talked with any of them since they had lunch earlier last week. Well back then, he was sure he'd be in church Sunday.

Max's husband answered the phone. "Hey, Tony. How you doing?" Josh asked.

"Pretty good, brotha. Missed you in church today," Tony answered.

"Yeah, man. Had a last-minute project come up at work. You know how that goes."

"Oh yeah, man, but you know the girls talked about you for a while. They gave you the blues. They swore you were with your new girl. You know they're all just jealous. Don't want you but don't want nobody else to have you. You know them. I tried to get them off your back, brother, but not even two of me can match up with one of them. Man, don't you leave me by myself with all of them again," Tony joked.

"I hear you, man. Thanks. That's why I'm calling now, to get my lashing and clear the slate, and to make contact with the human life form," Josh responded.

"Another one of your drops from existence? Man, that shit is so wild, but I understand. Max isn't here though. She stayed with the others after church. I came back home after we ate to watch the games. They said they would call you. By now, they're probably turning over every rock in the city trying to hunt you down."

"Yep, I might as well poke my head out now. They're bound to find me anyway. Thanks, man, for having my back. I know that was a futile battle."

"Hey, bruh, no problem. Good luck," Tony wished Josh.

"Yeah, really. All right, man. You take care. Holler at you later."

"All right then, man. Peace."

They hung up, and Josh realized he left out the house so quickly that he never checked his voice messages, so he called to retrieve his messages. He had about twenty-five new messages. The first eight were Carla, regarding their date Friday night. They started out sweet, then she got increasingly annoyed. Her last message said she was on her way over "to see why in the hell" he wouldn't call her back. "And it better not be no girl over there."

A couple of the fellas called to see what was up for the weekend. Some of them were balling Saturday at the recreation center. The others were going out Saturday night, clubbing. Chan called to see how he was doing and remind him about church on Sunday. Josh's mom called to tell him she was cooking a pot roast with all the fixings, and she baked an apple pie. Janessa called to see how he was getting along with the proposal and to warn him not to work too hard. The girls called after church to find out what Josh's problem was and have him meet them at their regular brunch spot. The girls called again and told him he better not let that floozy turn him into a heathen, and if she wouldn't come to church with him or at least make sure he went, then she wasn't worth the salt in bread.

Later on, they called to tell Josh they were going to 31's after they finished shopping and to meet them there if he could. That was the call Josh was looking for. Something was happening now, so he could comingle with people and reconnect to life again. He gave himself a curfew of midnight because he knew he would be working late tomorrow. Since it wasn't too late yet, Josh called his mother and told her he would come by and eat dinner. He wanted to make sure she wouldn't put the food away and have her expect his arrival. He didn't like the idea of his mom answering the door at night if she wasn't expecting someone.

# Max

MAX SAT IN CHURCH, WONDERING if the pastor had been given a script on the recent events in her life. It seemed instead of a sermon, he was talking directly to her. He always had a knack for doing that. It wasn't uncommon for many persons of the congregation to express those exact sentiments. "I felt like pastor Lacy was talking right to me."

Pastor Lacy had a powerful voice and the wonderful talent of teaching. He captured your attention and fed you with information that made you hunger for more. He didn't spend a lot of time on pomp and circumstance. He simply introduced the scripture subject and related it to history and current day realities. Basically, he had a way of telling it like it is while uplifting, educating, and giving hope.

This wasn't the first time Max experienced this feeling while sitting in church nor did she expect it to be the last, but this particular time, he was closer to home than usual. He tapped into a subject that was a current topic in her home.

"Lord, why you doing this to me?" the pastor mocked. "Why not you?" he answered his own question. "Folk always running around blaming God for the things going wrong in their lives. You can't find the *l* from *Lord* in their vocabulary when things are going right.

"Women have men who beat them, mistreat them. Men have women who sleep around, use drugs. And there they go. 'Lord, you done me wrong. I don't deserve this.' Don't blame God for your choices. That's what free will is all about. You made that decision to be with that fool. Even if you didn't find out until later in the relationship, why you still there? Choices. In fact, you're lucky God doesn't give you what you deserve!" The pastor paused to let that reality sink in.

The congregation chuckled, and the "Amen," "Ain't that the truth," "Say it," "Teach," and "Yes, Lord," poured out. Members of the church twisted and readjusted themselves in their seats, fanned themselves, and looked around, hoping no one had recognized the guilt on their faces about the pastor's last statement. They were even more disturbed at the thought of the Lord giving them what they deserved, knowing the sin they've committed and tried to cover up, hide, or ignore.

"And, sistahs, you walk around here moaning about you can't find a good man. Why God send you that trifling ole idiot who took all your money? You the one claimed that man. Dress smooth, talk smoother. You couldn't do without him. At least that's what you told yourself. Even with all the warning signs and alarms going off. 'Girl, but he so tall and fine…I know he ain't no good, but…he said he would…' God sent you the one who made dinner reservations, picked you up on time, and opened your car door. The one who said your money was no good that night.

The one who walked you to your door after the date and didn't try to come in. The one who sent you flowers a couple of days later, just because. The one you wouldn't call back anymore. The too short, too fat, too dark, too square one. The one you need but don't want. The one *you* didn't deserve. Stop blaming my Father for your choices!" the pastor scorned.

"And those of you who got a hold of a good one, stop taking their kindness for weakness. Compromise with your mate. For once, let them have their way, their request, their happiness. Cut out all the 'That's just the way I am' junk. Never giving in, never trying to understand them. Selfish. Just selfish. Don't say a thing when you finish pushing them to somebody who will share. There you go. Back to square one. 'Lord, why me?'"

The more the pastor went on, the deeper Max entered into that zone of being the only person in the church, with Pastor Lacy speaking and pointing his finger at her. All the "Amen" and "Say it, preacher" started fading. Soon she heard no more sound and found herself enveloped in a one-on-one counseling session. Once again, he gave her food for thought. Pastor Lacy quite possibly could have saved her marriage right at that very service without ever knowing it.

As he continued on, she vowed she would do better by Tony. Lord knows she loved him, but maybe she was being a little selfish and taking him for granted. She would have an in-depth conversation with him soon and do some things differently. Tony never tried to change Max, but now she wanted to change herself. He always said he was happy with whatever she wanted and would accept and love her regardless of her stubborn ways. She believed Tony and was pretty confident he wouldn't leave her simply for being stubborn.

*But what if he did?* Max thought, alarmed. *I couldn't stand to lose Tony. And certainly not over something I could have controlled.*

Max slowly faded back amongst the rest of the congregation as Pastor Lacy brought his sermon to a close. The congregation clapped and stood to their feet. The deacons and ministers in the pulpit patted the pastor on the back and gave him hugs and praises for another wonderful lesson. At the direction of the minister of music, the choir chimed in an encore upbeat rendition of "God Is Trying to Tell You Something" by Tata Vega.

Everyone began to exit the sanctuary and gather at various parts of the church, the parking lot, and the streets. They greeted and talked with familiar faces and smiled at not so familiar faces.

In those streets, Max, Tony, Chan, and Dede looked around for Josh, thinking he probably arrived late and sat in the balcony after not being able to find them. His face never surfaced. Tony told the group they'd better get going to brunch before it got too crowded, and he didn't want to miss too much of the game.

After breakfast, Max kissed Tony goodbye so he could catch his games and she could catch the malls. She was going to do a little shopping with the girls. Chan needed some black pumps for the sergeant interview she had coming up. Dede wanted to get some more matte foundation.

She hated running out, and her supply was getting low. Max said there was always something she could use or would find. They were going to drive out to the shops at Buckhead mall in Atlanta, Georgia.

They decided they would limit their spending and time in the mall that day. They wanted to eat, dance, and hang out a little at 31's, a funky, little happy hour jazz spot on Peachtree Street that incorporated some R & B for a good time. First, they drove over to 31's to park one of their cars so they could ride to the mall together. They left Josh a message telling him they would be at the club around six or seven o'clock.

Max had made up her mind that she wouldn't stay too late. She wanted to get home and hug Tony and have that heart-to-heart talk with him. She would leave no later than ten o'clock. She would surprise him because he knew she usually wouldn't get home until after midnight when she was shopping and hanging with the girls.

Josh got to the club at about eight thirty. Max had been ready to go, but she didn't want to spoil the others' fun. She was having a good time also, as usual. They always enjoyed themselves at 31's. It was such a lively yet mature crowd. Tonight, something just kept her thinking about home and getting to Tony. Since Josh arrived, Max decided to stay a little longer so they could talk with him, considering they hadn't heard from him in days. She asked him if he would drop her at home about nine thirty because she needed to talk to Tony before it got too late.

"Sure, Max. Is everything okay?" Josh asked, concerned.

"Yeah, it's cool. I just miss him tonight." Max smiled.

"Oooh, that's so cute," Chan teased.

"You can take my car," Dede offered. "Chan or Josh can bring me to pick it up when we leave."

"That'll be perfect. That way, I don't have to interrupt anyone's groove," Max said.

"Like you really cared with your horny self. All you know is you are feeling that man, and you wanna get to him." Chan unveiled Max's secret.

"Well, that's true, but still, I didn't want to be a party pooper," Max surrendered.

"It's cool, Max. Go home and take care of that man like you supposed to. It's only right," Josh interjected. "I spoke with him earlier. He sounded a little tense. Like he needs some attention."

"Oh yeah? What did he say?" Max asked.

"Nothing really. Just that you guys were sweating me hard," Josh emphasized.

"Oh, well, you deserved it. Dede, I have that spare key you gave me the other day, so I don't have to take yours. That way, you don't have to disturb us. Hint, hint." Max returned to the subject.

"Oh no. Hold up! She got a key to the Lexus?" Chan asked, jealous. "Where is mine? What? You don't trust me?"

"Chan, please," Dede said, giving her the hand to talk to. "How many emergency keys do you think I need out there. Besides, can't nobody ever catch up with your ass with the hours and shifts you work."

"Well, I just wanna feel the love too," Chan whined playfully.

"Awww," the girls said in unison and group-hugged Chan.

"You guys are really too much," Josh said, breaking up the moment. "Where's Kelly?"

"She called last night and said she had to take care of something, and she didn't think she'd be at service this morning," Max answered.

"I thought you two were together," Dede hinted.

"Oooh no you didn't, girl?" Chan asked.

"She did. You know she did," Max answered.

"Let's get a drink and groove a little before Max takes off," Josh changed the subject.

"Sounds like a plan to me. We already ate. Josh, do you need to order something? You know drinking on an empty stomach makes for a bad after-party," Dede said.

"No, I'm cool. I stopped and ate at my mom's house before I came here. C'mon, I got the first round," Josh responded.

Max got home sometime before ten o'clock. The house looked empty. She parked in the driveway so Dede could get to her car easily when she came to pick it up. She wondered if Tony was home. Neither of their cars were in the driveway. The house was quiet and dark; not one light on.

He usually left a hall light or a night-light on somewhere for her. Max was getting disappointed because she had so much to share with him, but he must have gone out. Before Max went upstairs, she went through the laundry room to peek in the garage and see if his truck was gone. Both cars were there. Unless he left with one of his friends, he must be upstairs sleeping.

Max took off her clothes downstairs. She wanted to slip into bed with her husband without waking him before her cool body touched his warm body. Max always wore sexy matching underclothes. She wanted to be able to excite Tony whenever and wherever her clothes were removed by him. It also made her feel good to dress from the inside out. She kept her body dressed in bath oils or lotions, matching her perfume *du jour*, usually Grand Soir by Maison Francis Kurkdjian of Paris, her favorite. Tony liked her supple, voluptuous body. He always commented on how soft she is.

Max tiptoed upstairs in her camisole and matching bikinis. She ducked into the bathroom when she saw light from the room after she got to the top of the stairs. Max grabbed a barrette, gathered her hair up loosely to the center of her head, and pinned it up. She started back on her journey to their room. The TV was on. Tony was still awake. Max startled him when she walked up to the bedroom.

"Hey, baby." Max glowed as she stood in the doorway.

Tony's heart skipped a beat. He didn't realize Max had come home. He took one look at his darling wife posing and her lack of clothing and sat straight up in the bed. He pulled the cover back and positioned himself at the edge of the bed. He held out his hand and beckoned Max to come to him. The spotlight followed Max as she stepped up to him with her hand out to meet his hand. Tony took Max into his arms and hugged her so strongly and gently. Max enveloped herself in the safety of his arms. Those brief moments of insecurity that Tony might love her any less were erased immediately. He lifted Max into his warm spot in the bed and blanketed her with the warmth of his body.

"Tony?" Max called sweetly.

"Yes, baby," Tony answered attentively.

"I need to talk to you about something," Max said with a tender edge of seriousness.

Tony rolled over and propped himself against the headboard. "Of course, baby. Is everything okay? You sound real disturbed."

"Yeah, I just been thinking. I've been kinda selfish…"

"About what? With who?" Tony quizzed with ample concern.

"With you. You know how we've talked about having a baby? And how you want a kid, and I didn't really?" Max hinted around.

"Yeah, but I told you I wouldn't bring it up again. We'd wait until you were ready, should you ever desire to have any, and I haven't. You know I will love you no matter what disagreements we may have. I know we will eventually get past them."

"I know, sweetie, and I love you too. But I never intended to have any children. Now or ever. I knew how important a child was to you, but I just didn't want to have one. I liked our relationship the way it was. I figured a kid would intrude on my time, our time, together. I wanted you all to myself. Knowing how deeply you felt about a child, I thought they would get all your attention. I didn't want to share."

"Baby, of course, I'm gonna love our child immensely. I think I have enough love to share so you won't feel neglected in that department."

"I know that theoretically, but I kept choosing to see it differently. I'd give all these excuses and reasons why I didn't want to have a child, why we shouldn't have one, but I realized denying you something you feel so passionately about is eventually going to drive you away."

"I'd never leave you, Max," Tony tried to reassure her.

"I know, baby. You'd never plan to leave me or intentionally do anything to hurt me, but my actions would sooner or later force your hand. I'd hate myself knowing I ran you away for pure selfishness."

"Max, it would be selfish of me to leave you because of something only I wanted. I knew before I married you how you felt about having children. I love you. I don't want to change you. I'm in it for the duration." He tried to comfort her with words. He could tell something was truly weighing on Max's mind.

"I love you so much, Tony. I have no justified reason to continuously take and not give. I want to share, compromise."

"What are you saying, Max?" Tony got curious.

"That after ten years of marriage, I've had plenty of time to have you to myself, and there will be plenty of time after they're away in college and grown up."

"Max, what exactly are you saying?" Tony asked again, getting excited inside. "*They* who?"

"Jeremy, Sasha, Bailey, Little Tony. I want us to have a baby too!" she announced.

"Really, Max? Are you sure?" Tony could hardly contain himself. "I don't want you to do anything you don't want to. Not just for me. You know I love you no matter what."

"I'm sure. I've been mulling this over for a while now, but I really made up my mind today. I love this baby so much already. Just the thought of it, knowing I have another part of you."

Tony cupped Max's face with both hands on each side of her cheek and gave her a big juicy smack on the lips. "See why I love you? Even when things are great, you give a little more of yourself to make them even better," Tony said, looking into her eyes.

Max just hugged his waist tightly and laid her head in Tony's chest. When he squeezed back, tears welled up in Max's eyes.

Max and Tony decided they would wait until the beginning of the new year before they would focus on Max getting pregnant. They wanted to put away some money for the planned new addition. Tony wanted to start preparing the third room for the baby. He always wondered what they would do with four bedrooms and no children. Only so much space can be used for an office or indoor gym. The third room was filling up with items they were too lazy to put away in the garage.

Max would have to have her Novis birth control device removed some time soon. She made an appointment for a month later to see her gynecologist. She wanted to inform him of their plans and get checked to make sure she was healthy enough for pregnancy.

Max smiled as she stared at the walls of her living room, admiring her impeccable taste in art and the amazingly skillful talent of the artist. She had several works by the young artist Jon Toms who originated from Denver. She was attracted to his faceless method of capturing the sound of music through vivid colors and floating ties. Max enjoyed supporting the uplifting and unity of black people via the arts, whether it was on canvas, dance and theater, or crafts. As Max continued to stand around her living room, she felt proud of her accomplishments but felt the need to try and enjoy the fruits of all that hard work a little more. She thought about her need to simply sit around her non-conventionally furnished living room and enjoy doing nothing. Her eccentric style and layout of furniture seemed to perfectly reflect who she was. No two pieces matched and there were no sets of anything, yet everything fit wonderfully in its place and exuded an aura of a loving family of the nineties. Just as most households use their living rooms for anything but living, Max's was no exception. It was more of a sitting room and a museum of cultural and ethnic artifacts and personal mementos.

In the southeast corner of the sitting room was a rectangular window that extended from the floor to the ceiling and had about ten separated panes. Below the window was a goose down chaise lounge with burgundy and earth tone stripes and extremely plush and comfortable pillows—the perfect spot for reading, chilling, or napping. Sitting directly adjacent to the chaise was a bookcase, Max's favorite piece of furniture because it embraces the items that so frequently sent Max through emotional roller-coaster rides. From that area alone, she has faced confusion, tears of joy, tears of sorrow, anger, happiness, and laughter. These items, her precious jewels, entertained Max thoroughly. She could read for hours. Max sat and wondered what's the sense in having these things, working hard, traveling all over, and creating and learning these wonderful stories of life, but having no one to share it with. A plethora of knowledge and wit, and no one with whom to pass it down. Now she would—her own flesh and blood.

Max went to work Monday, feeling refreshed and ready to take on the day's ups and downs. Max ran an exclusive quaint café and food bar that sat in the lobby of the Argyle building. Max's food bar, It's All Good!, is a modern architectural room with a marble rust-colored bar counter with four chrome bar stools. The tables and chairs were chrome with frosted glass tops and acrylic seats. The rest of the room was white with delicate art and plants scattered about. It looked like a doctor's office with style and energy.

It was clean and comfortable. Max made sure it wasn't one of those holes-in-the-wall where you endured the substandard surroundings just because the food was good. The atmosphere was good, and the food was better. It was a small but really classy joint. It barely held four tables and sets of chairs for the lunch goers. It had a patio area that made the atmosphere even more inviting and helped Max accompany the lunch crowd. The patio sat out over the stairs rising on a hill. It overlooked the courtyard, which had a beautiful fountain with a surrounding garden and Victorian statues. This made Max's café a prime location.

Whenever summer jazz concerts, company events, or simply beautiful days took place, her patio was the best seat in the house. You could see and hear everything without interruption. Max loved this place. She worked hard and got minimal return, but it was all worth it to her and Tony to have that sense of accomplishment and self-motivation. She only had two employees—the waitress and the assistant cook. She did an awful lot of the extra work to keep overhead cost low. Max barely made as much money as she did when she worked in the mainstream. She sometimes made less and worked harder. She figured it would all pay off in the long run. In the meantime, the feeling of being her own boss was payment enough. Max was the cook, cashier, clerk, and bookkeeper. For some things, she contracted outside when it was business smart and economically feasible.

Max always wanted her own business, and she knew she was a good cook and would follow along that path when she went into business. She took business courses, attended seminars, and researched the restaurant business. She prepared business plans in her classes and had them ready for when the right time and opportunity came. Max can recall vividly when she learned a space at the Argyle building became available, and they were taking bids and proposals for a service-oriented business. When she discovered the article in one of the local business papers she was reading during her lunch, she got frantic. There was only one day left to submit a bid.

She folded the paper, zipped over to the Argyle building purchasing department, and got a bid package. Max went back to work and took the rest of the day off. She went home and gathered her business plans in order to decide which one better fit the requirements of Argyle's bid conditions. Max spent the rest of the day completing the package. When Tony came home, they went over her offer. After they finished, Tony contacted one of his coworkers, Mitch, who was an accounts manager in the purchasing department at the utility company. Mitch had them email a copy of the proposal so he could review it for the important items that purchasing divisions look for when evaluating bids. He made changes on verbiage in certain areas. He said that should help get the attention of the bid officer and flag the executives that the prospective bidder has some experience in those type of dealings.

Mitch sent the copy back to Tony and wrote a note telling him good luck and to contact him if there was anything else he could do for them and let him know about the outcome of the bids. Max stayed up all night making the corrections, reviewing her offer, and proofreading her business plan. Tony finally talked her into coming to bed. He knew she'd be up again at the crack of dawn worrying about the bid and waiting for Purchasing to open. He knew how excited and extreme Max could be when she got her mind set on doing something.

The clerk opened the door to the purchasing division and had barely made it back behind the counter before Max was standing there smiling.

"I know this is last minute. I hope it doesn't count against me," Max said, inquiring to the clerk.

"No, ma'am. Everyone gets the same consideration as long as they make it in before the deadline. The deadline for this package is three o'clock today, so you're okay," the clerk responded. The clerk stamped Max's package, clocked in the receipt, and gave her a copy. "We will contact you in about four to six weeks regarding the outcome and the package selected."

"Do you know if there are other ways to get information on open bids for service-offered businesses? Is there a mailing list or something that would give me faster notice?" Max asked.

"Other companies may have that service, but you'd have to check with them individually. We don't offer the notification through mail service. Unfortunately, you'd have to come in and check our bulletin board behind you regularly or check our website for updates. We do print a fact sheet that lists recent bids weekly until they close and, of course, the public notice ads."

"Oh, thanks for your help. I really appreciate it," Max said sincerely.

"You're welcome, and good luck."

Max floated out the purchasing office. She danced inside while she waited for the elevator. She had taken another serious step toward achieving that dream of being an entrepreneur. She was jazzed. Max gave her smile to every eye she caught and followed it with a warm hello. Just knowing she was now a real contender in fulfilling her dream made her feel good. Max had gotten into the arena. Even if this one didn't work out in her favor, she had a renewed determination and knew something would work eventually. She was motivated and ready to take on the task of pursuing her goal.

Max went on to work and tried to continue business as usual. She didn't want to think too much about the offer. She knew six weeks of constant wondering and counting the days would make her absolutely dizzy.

When Max received the letter regarding her bid offer at the Argyle building, she didn't know what she was open-ing. She thought it was basically junk mail, some finance company or something soliciting for loans. The return address had Stein and Black Ltd. Max pulled out the letter, prepared to skim through it and throw it away. She began to read: "Mrs. Staten, this letter is regarding your recent proposal to the Argyle building for a food-service business in their lobby. We received many viable bids, and it was a difficult decision."

Max's heart paused when she realized she was reading the letter she had been waiting on for months. She looked around over her shoulder real quick for Tony, but he wasn't near. She took a seat at the dining room table so she could read further. *Yeah, but what was your decision?* Max thought to herself. She was getting anxious.

"As a part of a program designed to extend opportunity to minority business persons and our need for a food-service company, we were able to narrow our decision down considerably."

Max didn't want to get too happy too quickly, but it sure sounds like the odds were in her favor and her chances had increased. She always said she would stand in any line of opportunity. The female minority line, the black minority line, the low-income minority line, whatever line. If it meant her getting an opportunity she otherwise would not have, she'd stay in line all day. Right now, she just wished this letter would get to the point. If she didn't breathe soon, it wouldn't matter what the decision was; they'd be having her funeral.

"We would like to extend our congratulations to you for your selection as the new contractor in the Argyle building, for bid S-761. Please contact our offices for further information and your acceptance of this selection."

Max screamed, "*Eeiooow!* Tony!" She ran through the house with the letter in her hand, frantically looking for Tony. She ran past him twice. He was in the spare room looking for one of his tools. He finally stepped out in the hallway so he could intercept her on her next flight past him. "I got it! I got it! They accepted my proposal!" Max shouted.

Tony looked at Max for a split second and grabbed her to give her a big giant hug. "Congratulations, baby. I'm so proud of you." He held her by the shoulders and looked straight into her eyes. "I knew you could do it."

Max hugged him back. "We did it. We did it."

"No, *you* did it," Tony told her. "Now what do you have to do next?"

"I don't know really. They said to call them for further information and to accept this selection. Oooh, I better call now." Max started toward the telephone.

"Baby, they're probably closed. It's after six o'clock," Tony said tenderly, not wanting to burst Max's bubble.

"Oh yeah, I guess so. Well, I'll just call first thing in the morning," Max said, sobering.

"Let's go out and celebrate," Tony told Max.

"Okay." Max looked down at herself. "Do I need to change clothes?"

"No, you look good already. Let's go."

Tony took Max to dinner and dancing. They called Mitch and told him and his wife to join them if they could. It was impulsive and spontaneous, but they had the time of their lives. Max wore everyone out on the dance floor. Mitch's wife told Max to take Mitch out there on the floor cause he was wearing her out, trying to keep up with Max and Tony. It also looked like Max had worn Tony out. Tony and Helen sat down to catch their breath. It wasn't long before Max wore Mitch down as well. They settled down to chat and laugh the rest of the night away.

When they left, Max told Tony it was the most fun she had in a long time. She said the night was perfect because she would not have been able to sleep if she stayed home. Now she was pooped and would have to wait and share her excitement with everyone later on.

The nurse called. "Maxine Staten?"

"Yes?" Max stood and walked toward the voice.

The nurse smiled at the familiar face and opened the door wider so Max could enter the examining area. She pointed toward the end of the hall. "You know where to go."

"Yeah, I know, to that ole evil weight machine," Max teased.

Max stepped out of her shoes and onto the scale. Max preset the weights for the nurse to save herself the embarrassment of the nurse inching the weight up on the bar. To her surprise, the bar didn't balance. It fell down. She had lost weight! By that time, the nurse arrived and began inching the weight down. Max watched with pleasure. She had lost seven pounds. The nurse picked up Max's file to write down her weight, and she noticed the difference from the last entry.

She asked, "Are you on a diet? You've lost weight since your last visit."

"No. I don't know how that happened, but I'm sure glad it did. As long as I'm not sick. I don't really feel like I'm losing weight," Max responded.

"Oh, that's interesting. Well, why are you here today?" the nurse asked.

"My period has been strange the last couple of times. This time, it was real scanty. I only spotted for about two and a half days, and I've been feeling sluggish lately. I don't know if it's a reaction from having the Novis removed or if I'm coming down with the flu or something. Maybe that's why I'm losing weight."

"It could be both. We'll let the doctor examine you and see what's going on." The nurse showed Max to an examining room and handed her a gown. "Remove all your clothes and put this on. The doctor will be with you shortly."

The doctor tapped on the door and entered while looking down reading Max's file. "You're back rather soon. I don't see any problems with your lab results. What brings you in today?"

"My period has been weird, and for the last couple of days or so, I've been feeling weird too."

"Have you had a period this month?"

"Yes. But it only lasted about two days, and I just spotted the whole time."

"What about the one before this one?"

"I bled fairly regular, but it was short too. Maybe three to four days. Does this happen when you stop birth control?"

"It could. The body could have varying reactions, but it doesn't usually make you sick or anything like that. Have you been nauseous?"

"No, just tired lately," Max responded.

"Lie down. I'm going to do a pelvic examination. When I finish, I'm going to order blood and urine sample for testing." The doctor called for his nurse to assist him with the exam and told her to get a blood and urine sample after he finished. "Your stomach feels hard. When did we remove the birth control device?" the doctor asked.

The nurse picked up the chart to look up the date, and Max responded, "About three months ago. Is that supposed to happen?"

"It depends. Let me get the results from your samples, and we'll go from there. I'll be back shortly after the results come back. You can put your clothes back on."

Max was waiting about fifteen minutes before the doctor came back to the room with his findings. "Well, to answer your question, yes, it's supposed to happen, if you're pregnant. And, my dear Mrs. Staten, you are pregnant."

Max looked at the doctor with her mouth open and without blinking. "Excuse me?"

"You're pregnant. I'd guess about six weeks or so. I'll have to do an ultrasound to better determine the date of conception. In the meantime, I'll get you started on some vitamins and iron supplements. Make an appointment to get an ultrasound and begin your prenatal care. Congratulations. Maxine?"

"Yes?" Max replied.

"Close your mouth. I remember just a couple of months ago you were in this office saying this is what you wanted," the doctor teased.

"Oh yeah, I did. I mean, I do. I mean…," Max stammered.

"Relax. Everything will be just fine. Start on those vitamins, eat healthy, and you'll get your energy back. See you in three weeks."

The doctor left the room, and Max continued to sit on the examining table, stunned. They planned to have a baby but not right now. That was the furthest thing from her mind when she walked into the doctor's office. She expected it would be a little difficult for her to get pregnant. In the back of her mind, she believed she couldn't get pregnant. Evidently, she could. She was just lucky those other times when she didn't use any birth control. Max laughed, "I'll be damned. Tony's gonna be a daddy. I'm gonna be a mommy. And I thought I had the flu." She leaned back and cracked up.

The nurse came in. "Mrs. Staten? You okay?"

"Oh yes. Just fine." Max stepped down and gathered her belongings.

"Don't forget to make your appointment at the front desk," the nurse told Max as she left the examining room.

"Okay. Bye. Take care. See you in three weeks." Max was giggling.

On her way back to the café, Max had a million things running through her mind. *Should I take off the rest of the day? Go see Tony and tell him, or wait until tonight? Should I call the girls? When do I start telling folks? Do I wait until I'm showing? Wow, I'm already almost two months! Oh my God, but I've lost weight. Is there something wrong? Am I too old to have kids? I'm gonna get so fat. Should I start exercising? Do I need maternity clothes? Oh, another reason to shop. Not yet, silly. Slow down. You didn't even know you were pregnant! Whew! I need a drink. Oh, but I can't. Little missy doesn't need any bad habits already. Oh no! Have I had a drink in the last two months? All right, all right, Max. Stop tripping. You're just having a baby. Cut the drama. Yeah, but it's my baby.*

Max pulled into the parking garage and pushed the elevator button for the lobby as she wondered what she would name the baby.

"Hi, Mrs. Staten," the waitress said when Max walked in. "It got really busy this afternoon, about a half hour after you left, but everything went fine. There must have been something going on at the Argyle building because there has been constant traffic through here today. A lot of new faces."

"I'm sorry I left you guys alone for so long, especially since it got so busy. I didn't hear about any scheduled events or programs today."

"Oh no, it was no problem. We like it when it's busy, right? Busy is a good thing. Busy is our friend. Anyway, you look happy. Everything must have gone well at the doctor's office today."

"Yeah, a pretty clean bill of health. I'm not really sick. I just have to start taking vitamins and take better care of myself, give my body a little pep," Max said.

"That's good. You really do look happy. Like you could walk on water. Like you're glowing or something."

"I feel like I could do a lot of things, but we know only my Father has skills for that water walking stuff," Max laughed as she walked to the kitchen.

The waitress giggled along with Max and went to check on a customer sitting at one of the tables in the back.

It really had been a busy day at work. She had to help the waitress the entire day. She didn't get to take care of any of the business duties during the shift. All the cleaning, shelving, clearing the cash register, stocking the coffee pots, preparing the menu had to wait to the end of the day. She also had to go to the night depository. Max didn't like keeping large sums of money at the café or on her person. Luckily, the bank was in the building next door. Whenever she worked late, one of the security officers would walk with her to the bank and her car. She called the dispatch office and told the desk sergeant she was leaving and asked if there was anyone available to walk her down. When Officer Jones arrived, Max had just turned off all the lights and was gathering her keys and belongings to leave.

"Hi, Michael. How you doing?" Max called out as she stepped out the door and began locking up.

"Fine, Mrs. Staten. How are you?"

"Pretty good, thanks. I need to walk over to the bank and make this drop. Do you mind?" Max asked.

"Oh, no trouble at all. It's a nice night out. I could use a little walk. You ready?" the officer asked.

"Yep, all done. Let's go," Max said.

Tony got home before Max. He was in the den watching the game. Max got home considerably later than usual. She walked into the den and spoke to Tony. "Hey, baby."

Tony looked up. "Hey you, how did it go today?"

"Fine. How was your day?" Max asked.

"Fine. Same ole stuff, different day. You're home late. Busy day?"

"Yep."

"Did you make it to the doctor?"

"Yep." Max sat in Tony's lap, looking dreamingly into his eyes.

"Did everything go okay?"

"Yep," Max said.

Tony kissed Max's forehead and chuckled. "You're being awfully goofy today. What's going on, Max?" In the same instance Tony asked the question, his attention was shifting back to the TV. His team was about to score a touchdown.

"You're about to be a daddy. I'm pregnant," Max responded.

Tony leaped out of his seat and threw his hands straight in the air. Max plopped to the floor, right on her butt.

"Yes! Oooh, I'm sorry, baby. Are you okay?" Tony bent down to help Max up.

Max was laughing. "Yes, I'm all right. Are you cheering for that touchdown or the baby?"

Tony was patting Max's stomach, worried. "Are you sure you're okay? Really, Max, you're pregnant?" Max nodded. Again, Tony threw his hands up. "Yes!" He grabbed Max and gave her a big hug. "Here, baby, sit down." Tony was holding her stomach and back as he led her to the couch.

"Tony, I'm not about to deliver right now. I'm fine," Max chuckled.

"Are you sure you're okay? Did that hurt?"

"Well, yeah." Max rubbed at her butt. "But I'm okay though."

"When? How? Well, I know how, but you know what I mean," Tony asked.

"I'm almost two months."

"Wait, what! That was quick," Tony said, surprised.

"I know. It shocked me too. I know we didn't plan to really start trying until next year. Are you sure you're okay about this?"

"Am I okay? Girl, I've been okay with this since I met you! I'm just surprised it happened now. We weren't even trying. That was the last thing I expected you to say to me."

"Me too, but now I'm so excited. I go back to the doctor in three weeks to get an accurate measurement of how many weeks I am. Honey, I don't think I want to tell anyone until I'm about four months or starting to show," Max said.

"Why, Max? You scared?"

"No, I feel pretty good about everything. I know everyone is gonna get all excited and want this baby to be born tomorrow, and this pregnancy will end up taking forever," Max responded.

"I see. I don't know if I can hold it in for that long. Maybe you shouldn't have told me yet either," Tony teased.

"I know. I thought about that," Max responded.

"Girl, I was just kidding. You better not have kept this from me. I still don't know if I'm able to keep it a secret, but I'll try. You know how long my mother has been waiting to hear this news?" Tony said.

"I know, I know," Max said with the understanding that Tony never could hold water.

# Kelmax

MAX PULLED INTO KELLY'S DRIVEWAY. A sense of extreme sadness came down on her. She knew whatever it was Kelly wanted to tell her would not be good news. She had no idea what it could be, but somehow, she knew it was serious. Max took her time gathering her things before she got out of her car. She wanted to compose herself. She did not want to knock at the door all sad and pitiful and make things worse before Kelly had a chance to talk to her. Besides, if it was indeed bad news, she needed to be the ball of strength for Kelly. Max prayed Kelly's mother was okay. She didn't know how she could help Kelly if that was the case. Kelly would fall to pieces, and Max wouldn't be far behind her. Mrs. LeBeau always treated Max just like her daughter, and Max loved her dearly. Mrs. LeBeau was the mother Max never knew, and Kelly was the sister she never had.

Josh had left about thirty minutes earlier. He came to visit Kelly, but she told him she had asked Max over and needed to have a one-on-one talk with her. Josh understood and told Kelly he'd call her later that evening. He went out to play ball and run a few errands.

Max rang the doorbell and twisted the knob to open the door. She peeked in and called out to Kelly as she started walking into the house. Kelly was walking toward the front door, coming out of the kitchen. She was drying her hands on a kitchen towel after washing the few dishes she and Josh dirtied while they drank tea and ate the cinnamon rolls he brought with him.

"Hey, girl," Kelly called out.

Max smiled. "How you doing?"

"I'm fine. How about you?" Kelly asked as she hugged Max.

"Good. You look cute. What's up?"

"Thanks. Girl, it's a long story. Come on in. Grab a seat," Kelly responded with a sigh. "You hungry? Might as well be comfortable."

"Yeah, a little bit. What you got?" Max asked.

"You want breakfast or lunch? I got some fried chicken leftovers, or I could whip you up an omelet or something real quick."

"Have you eaten yet?" Max asked.

"Yeah, I had a cinnamon roll and tea earlier. I'm not too hungry." The phone rang, and Kelly went in the back to answer it.

"I'll just fix me a quick sandwich. That'll hold me, and I can't believe you still have a house phone," Max called out behind Kelly. Max kicked off her shoes. She went into the kitchen and began preparing herself a sandwich.

Kelly finished her phone call and turned the ringer off. She turned down the answering machine so she wouldn't be interrupted and walked back into the living room.

"Okay, so where was I?" she asked.

Max stepped into the living room with her sandwich and a tall glass of juice. She set out a coaster and placed the glass on top. She was already chewing a bite of her sandwich. "You were about to tell me a long story," Max told her.

"That's right." Kelly slapped her thighs and sighed. She was preparing herself to remain strong while she told this story. Max could see the uneasiness enter Kelly's eyes. She didn't want to let on that anxiety was written all over Kelly's face. Max showed concern and gave Kelly her undivided attention. Kelly started talking again. "Well, there really is no easy way to say this, so I'll just say it. Max, I have AIDS."

Max froze. This was not one of the scenarios she came up with when she tried to figure out what was so pressing with Kelly. The whole time she hoped it would be good news, and she would feel silly for thinking the worst. Everything ran through her mind.

Nothing ran through her mind. Nothing of value. Nothing of significance. Nothing intelligent enough to open her mouth and let out as a response. She was stunned. She was hurt. She was saddened. She was mad. She was dumbfounded. Max had failed her friend. She was completely unable to be that rock. That person who always knew just the right thing to say. The one who stood steadfast when everyone else broke. Max has withstood many blows and pacified others who faced trials and tribulations, yet now, when she was needed the most, she had nothing to say. She searched through the many thoughts and experiences in her head. There had to be some form of intelligent life in there somewhere. What is wrong with her? She had to be able to help. Her friend needed her. That's why she called, isn't it?

Max felt useless. She couldn't fix this. She couldn't say anything witty; point Kelly in the right direction or anything. Hell, she couldn't even speak. And look at Kelly. Stoic. The one who usually loses her mind. One extreme or the other—either frantic and mad as all get out or frantic and whiny. How can she be so strong? Max was crumbling by the second. She felt herself going to pieces.

"Girl, breathe!" Kelly exclaimed.

Max came out of her stupor. She refocused on Kelly and began to cry. Still no words. She just cried. She buried her face in her hands and cried like a baby. Kelly got up and stepped over to console her friend. "I'm sorry. I'm so sorry." Max sobbed with her face still in her hands and now the crown of her head in Kelly's chest.

"It's okay, girl. I understand," Kelly responded.

"I'm sure this doesn't help one bit. I'm so, so sorry," Max repeated.

"I know. I did the same thing. Many times. I don't think I have any tears left in me on this particular issue at this point," Kelly responded.

Max stood up and hugged her friend. She just hugged her and held on. Kelly began to shed a few light tears. It was the love she felt from her friend that made her cry. It saddened her to see Max feeling so worthless, so vulnerable, and she didn't know how to make that go away. They stayed there in that position for several seconds, heaving.

Max finally thought about the picture they portrayed and tried to wipe her face and regain her stature.

"Look at this. You consoling me, and you're the one with the unbearable news," Max said.

Kelly tried to laugh. "We are kind of pitiful, aren't we? Go in the bathroom, and clean yourself up." Max walked toward the bathroom, and Kelly went to the linen cabinet to get her a facecloth. Kelly walked into the bathroom behind Max and handed her the towel. "Girl, look at you. Just sad. All pitiful-looking. Big, Bad Max broke down," Kelly teased.

"I know. I feel so helpless. I don't know what to do," Max responded.

"Uh-uh, you helped so much. Just showing your true feelings let me know how deeply you care for me. How painful it is for you to feel like you can do nothing is help enough. Your unconditional love means more to me than any words. Come back out in the front when you're done, and we'll finish talking about this. I guess we never really got started, huh?"

"Yeah, really. I'll be right out," Max said.

Max came out of the rest room still looking like she was hit by a Mack truck, but she did manage to regroup and conjure up the strength she figured she needed to ingest the information her friend was about to share. Max first thought she could steady herself for the blow she was about to receive, and then she thought, how dare she think *she* was about to take a blow. Kelly took the full force of the blow without warning and without padding to cushion her fall from the knockout. Max sat down quietly, knowing there were no proper words or action to lighten the situation. She looked straight at her friend with an expression that told Kelly she was ready to listen.

Kelly sighed. "I'm not quite sure there is a particular beginning or end to this story. So I may just talk in circles and bounce around, but eventually, I will arrive to what I'm trying to tell you to my fullest understanding of the whole thing."

Max said nothing. She didn't know how to respond, and she wanted Kelly to be able to tell her story in her own way, without interruption.

Kelly continued, "I have full-blown AIDS. I found out about a year and a half ago. About a year and a half too late. I never even knew I was HIV positive. Unfortunately, it doesn't look good. During the time I've known, I've been prescribed various medications to stabilize me but without much success. My body hasn't responded to the medication. My T cells have yet to rise or stop dropping, for that matter. I continue to take them because it would be much worse without them. The drawback is it makes me violently ill. I get such bad headaches and so sick to my stomach that I get weak from heaving. Eventually, I'll end up taking about a hundred pills a day. Now you know I'm hating that, but if it helps, I guess I can deal with it."

"You have to take a hundred pills, Kelly?" Max asked with concern and disgust at the thought of taking that many pills.

"Not literally, Max, but I do take multiple pills, different ones at different times. So anyway, I figured I'd better share this news with you guys because I may start getting really sick in the near future. I mean, I feel okay now, so don't trip. It hasn't started taking a toll on my body yet. I haven't told anyone at work yet. I've been researching all the legal aspects regarding my rights in the workplace, should they decide to try and screw over me when I do tell them. Oh man, I know Ian is going to lose his entire mind when I tell him. He fusses over me like my mother."

"What can I do, Kelly? Anything you need? How can I help?"

"Girl, just keep loving me. Don't treat me any differently. And pray for my mom. This is gonna tear her apart. I need you to stay strong for us."

With a very slight gasp, Max responded, "That's right! Your mom. How is she taking this?"

"That's just it. I haven't told her yet. I'm gonna tell her and my brothers together. Speaking of helping me, you think you can be with me when I get ready to tell them? I don't know if I can handle it by myself."

"Ooh, that's true. It's gonna be interesting," Max said rather bleakly. "Of course, I will. Just let me know when you're ready to tell them."

"Thanks, Max."

Max became serious and somber. "How did you find out you have AIDS? You go in for routine testing?"

"No, not really. I never had an AIDS test before. I went because I was getting tired of that constant and recurring yeast infection. Since I was constantly complaining and started having mood swings and chronic fatigue, my doctor decided to run a full blood work."

"You never had an AIDS test?" Max asked with extreme surprise. "Why not?"

"Well, I never thought I had it. Or could have it. I mean, I've only had a couple of sex partners since college, and I always, *always*, used protection. Before that, Kevin was the only guy I had been with, so when I would think about HIV and the whole AIDS thing, I didn't consider my younger years, my college days. I felt I was acting responsibly about sex, and I had taken the precautions to make sure I didn't expose myself to HIV or AIDS. I learned my lesson well when Kevin fooled around on me. Unfortunately, my first lesson was my worst lesson."

"What do you mean?"

"I think I got it from my college days. From player, punk ass Kevin. That's what I believe. When I found out, it was already full-blown AIDS, not HIV, so I had to have had it for quite a while. At least ten years because, generally, the virus, HIV, stays dormant for a while, in most cases."

"What if it was someone else or if you gave it to someone else? I'm sorry. Am I asking too many questions?"

"No, no, no. I welcome questions. I've learned so much about sex, sexuality, and HIV since this discovery that I'd hate to die not having shared or educated someone to maybe save or prolong another life."

Max flinched when Kelly made reference to dying. Since they began this conversation, Max hadn't thought specifically about Kelly dying. Her basic knowledge of the disease was it was debilitating and destructive, but her mind blocked out the fact that she could soon lose Kelly to this illness. After all, Kelly did say she had full-blown AIDS. They'd have to face that inevitable fact.

Max softened her voice. "Kelly, are you thinking about dying?"

"In a way, yes. At first, that was all I thought about. I was living knowing I was dying, but that's no longer my focus. I can't unscramble those eggs, so I've adopted a new zest for life."

"Did you contact Kevin?"

"Yep. Well, not exactly. I tried, but he died of AIDS about four years ago. I don't know if he knew he was spreading the infection, and I guess I won't ever know."

"What? Damn, that is so deep. That's wild. So your first love messed you up for life! See, and folks run around persuading people to have sex and try all these new things, talking about it won't kill you. Hell, it just might!"

"I know, Max. I felt that same anger, cheated, but I'm not even tripping off that anymore. I just wish I could do something about how lackadaisical people are on the issue. That's what makes the cycle so vicious. They just aren't taking it seriously. I waited too late to pay attention to the public warnings, thinking it wouldn't happen to me, and now it's starting to hit black girls at younger and younger ages."

"But you're taking this so well. How can you be that optimistic about something so devastating?"

"I haven't been this way the whole time. I was angry. Mad as hell. Mad at everybody and everything. I was even mad at God. Wanted to know how he could do this to me. The worst part is I was mad but couldn't express my anger.

I had no outlets or any way to express my feelings because I was also ashamed. Ashamed at getting myself in this predicament and ashamed for letting my family and friends down. I finally went to talk with the pastor. He helped me remember my many blessing in life, then I connected with other AIDS survivors and counselors. It's helped considerably."

"So now what, Kel?" Max asked.

"I don't know. Same thing, I guess. Live everyday with as much intensity and happiness I can muster up. One other thing, Max. When time and opportunity presents itself, could you tell the others?"

"Girl, you sure you don't want to do that? You know I don't like telling other folks' business and all that gossiping mess."

"It's not gossiping unless you were being sneaky and vicious. I only want to have to tell this story once more, and that's to my mom and my brothers. I don't want to have to deal with everyone's first reaction. You know what I mean?"

"If you're sure."

"I'm sure. I just want them to know and hope they don't feel differently toward me. If they do, I'll get the message when I don't see them come around anymore. At least I won't have to see the disgust on their faces."

"I understand, but I don't believe they would trip like that. Before I tell anyone, I'll check with you again in about a week or so and see if you still feel the same."

"Suit yourself," Kelly responded apathetically. "So what do you want for lunch? I planned on making jambalaya."

"That's cool. I see you haven't changed. Still putting in serious work in that kitchen. You know they say the way to a man's heart is through his stomach, then your butt should have been married about six or seven times by now. Girl, you know you do some serious cooking, especially for a bachelorette," Max teased.

"You should talk. You're the one who put out Sunday feasts throughout the week. Like you're cooking for ten people. Ain't nobody but you and Tony."

"Yeah, but cooking is my profession. That's what I do. Besides, it used to work back then. That's how I got to Tony's heart. You know that man stays hungry."

"That's how you got to all our hearts. You think we were popping up at your house on Sundays because we like your company? Right."

"Oh, that's cold. And all this time, I thought you guys loved me. I guess it's true though. I remember how glad Josh was when I introduced him to you all. He had himself some partners in crime. He used to be a little hesitant to come by thinking he was intruding and Tony didn't appreciate it. I tried to tell that fool Tony was not thinking about him. He would call and ask what I cooked and have me bring leftovers to work. That nut would come clear across town to pick up his plate at lunch time, so once he met you guys, that was his ticket to get home-cooked meals directly from the oven to his palette."

"What? You mean he was using us?" Kelly asked surprised.

"Oh, look at you. Yeah, just like you used me, turkey."

"Okay, so it's like that now?" Kelly pretended to be hurt. "Hey, Max, remember when we met Chan and Dede?"

"Do I? How could I ever forget that? It was classic. I don't think we'll ever see anything like it again."

"Okay? There we were sitting at that cute little cozy café eating lunch and then we started hearing this quiet argument that was getting progressively louder going on behind us."

Max interrupted Kelly's storytelling. "Yeah, and your nosy ass decide you need to get a good look at the arguer and 'arguee.' What did you do that for? He started in on you, 'Bitch, what you looking at?' Oh no he didn't! Then you went, 'Motherfucker, I got your bitch! If you were any kind of man or had any damn sense, you wouldn't be in here threatening a woman with your punk ass.' That fool got heated."

"I know, huh? He must have thought he was a pimp or something. What was that he said? 'I made this bitch who she is, and I'll whip her ass, your ass, and that bitch's ass across the table from you!' And you talking about me? You lost your entire mind when he called *you* a bitch. 'You sorry-ass broke-dick bastard. Fuck the fuck out of you! It ain't that much ass whipping in all of Georgia.' Max, fuck the fuck out of you? Girl, were you mad or what? I ain't gonna ever forget that one as long as I live."

"Shut up," Max joked. "And while I'm jumping all bad, about to get my ass beat down, Dede standing over there all pathetic and whining at that guy. 'Frank, why you doing this? You don't even know them. Why are you talking to them like that? Calling them out of their name and stuff. That's why I can't be with you. Every time you get high, you start tripping.' He really didn't like her putting his business in the streets. She must have struck a nerve because he hauled off and slapped her into the middle of the next week."

"Oh, that's right, but who called the police? Chan walked in at the same time Dede got her clock cleaned."

"'Police! Sir, do not hit her again,' Chan asked with her baton in her hand."

"'Bitch, I'll kick your ass too. You hoes all the same. Try to get tough until somebody put you in your place. That's just what I'm gonna do. Put her ass in her place. When I'm done, I'll do the same to you if you don't get out my way,' Frankie threatened."

"'Sir, don't take another step. Put your hands up, and face the wall,' Chan requested calmly."

"'Fuck you,' Frankie responded, preparing to hit Dede again."

"He must have truly been high 'cause he was tripping big time. I don't know if it was the 'bitch' or the 'fuck you' that got to Chan, but she opened up a can of whoop ass on him. She leaped on that idiot before he knew what was what," Kelly laughed.

"She had him on the ground pounding his face to the floor until he put his hands up in submission. I saw you sneaking in those kicks to his back."

"Well, it was the 'bitch' that got to me," Kelly fessed up.

"You're stupid. Meanwhile, Dede still over there looking pitiful and crying, and your goofy butt just gonna make her be our friend. 'C'mon, let's get you cleaned up and get you something to eat. I know you're hungry. Look how skinny you are.' She tried to laugh a little. She sure perked up when you mentioned shopping. Why is that the answer to all our problems?"

"I don't know, but it worked on Chan as well. Remember we called the station and intruded in on her life too?"

"Yep, and we've been the Fab Five ever since."

"You remember that time on the plane when we were going to the Essence Festival in New Orleans?" Max surmised.

"Oh yeah. When that guy kept kicking your chair?"

"Yeah, he was sitting back there putting his feet up on the back of my seat like he was at home in a lounge chair. The bad part is he kept moving around. I'm sitting there like, no, he's not just beating on my seat like this. So, I reclined my seat so he'd get a clue someone was sitting there and he was disturbing them. Did he stop? Nooo. Now I'm really irritated. I looked around the seat at him and his feet in a way to give him another not-so-subtle hint of the discomfort he was causing me. He had the audacity to ask me, 'What is your problem?'"

"Yeah, he didn't know what he had gotten himself into. You leaped up in your chair, standing on your knees, leaning over the top of the seat, going off. 'You, sir. You are my goddamn problem. Why in the fuck are you kicking my seat like you're out of your goddamn mind? Like some kind of two-year-old. Did you pay fare for this seat too? I think not. If so, someone owes me a serious refund. If you need that much damn room, your cheap ass should have bought first class. If you continue to make my flight miserable and threaten my trust and safety in flying, I'll sue your ass. Think it won't happen, try me.' His wife, girlfriend, or whoever she was, was looking all stupid. Then you just sat down like you had just requested a cup of water or something. Everybody was all stunned and looking at him like, 'What did he do to her?' He was all molded and in shock. He didn't think you would go there on him. I wanted to bust up, but you were so mad and so serious that I just chilled. You know, they have laws against air rage. You took road rage to a whole new level."

By the time Max and Kelly finished reminiscing and laughing, the food was done. They ate and talked and laughed about old times some more. Before it got too late, they decided to do their favorite pastime—shopping and catching a movie.

When they got back to Kelly's place, Max offered again to stay over if Kelly needed her. "You sure you don't want me to stay? I can call Tony from here and let him know I'm staying."

"No. I keep telling you, I'm okay. And if you must know, so you'll take your ass home, I'm expecting company."

Max cut her eyes chaffingly at Kelly. "Well, excuse me, missy."

"Don't even start," Kelly laughed and got out of the car and said, "Call or text me when you get home."

# Chan

CHAN WAS HAVING ANOTHER INTENSE conversation with her son. One of many they've had in the recent months. Since reaching his teen years, Tyler has been a bit of a challenge. Like most parents with their teenagers, Chan was having a difficult time convincing him to be responsible and mindful of his future. Tyler has gotten to the point where all that matters is basketball and being a ladies man. He was frequently on the phone all day and evening and beginning to get home later and later on the premise of having basketball practice. Homework, housework, and everything else in between were being neglected. Chan decided she had watched this new development over the past few weeks long enough. Again, Tyler came in from practice late, got on the phone, and continuously ignored Chan's request for him to get off the phone and do his homework.

"Tyler, it's time to get off the phone," Chan called out. Chan continued to prepare herself for bed and get her clothes together for work. She dallied around the house a little longer, picking up, putting up, and throwing out things. She passed by the den and looked in and saw Tyler still on the phone. "Tyler, I said get off that phone. Do your homework and take a shower."

Chan went to her room and climbed into bed. She attempted to watch a little TV before she fell asleep. She got thirsty and went to the kitchen to get a glass of juice. When she passed the den again, she noticed Tyler was still on the phone. Chan went into the den and took his phone and hung it up.

"Mom, why you tripping? You just hung up in her face," Tyler asked, apparently upset.

"I don't care. I asked you to get off the phone several times an hour ago," Chan responded equally upset.

Tyler jumped up from his chair. "Man, you be tripping. I'm getting sick of you all up in my face, player hating."

By the time the words finished rolling off Tyler's lips, there was no opportunity for thought or retraction. Chan clinched her fist and bought it clear from Georgia on through Alabama, around Mississippi, across Louisiana, and into Tyler's chest. The shock and impact knocked him flat on his butt. He found himself looking up at his mother with his eyes glossy. Too proud, too much of a man, to cry.

"Boy, you think I'm some punk on the street or something?" Chan asked, enraged.

"Why you hit me?" Tyler asked surprised.

"You can do one of two things. Get up and do what I said or get up and get knocked down again. You must be out of your mind, thinking you can talk to me anyway you want. Walking around this house like you paying the bills, putting food on the table, and I'm the child! Jump up in my face like that again. Next time, you die," Chan promised.

Chan walked out. She forgot she was thirsty. She went to her room to recuperate. It drained and hurt her to be at this point with her son in their relationship. She sat in the dark thinking and found herself sobbing. She needed to talk to someone, do something. She tried to stop herself from crying so she could write in her journal; relieve some of the pain she was feeling.

When Tyler got up, he went to his room to get his backpack. He could hear his mother crying. He was still rubbing his chest. He was too angry with her to feel her pain.

*Daily Entry*
*03/21*

I had to hit my son tonight. I haven't had to touch him in over six or seven years. He's starting to forget what I taught him, as best I could, about being a man and how to treat a woman. He certainly forgot who the reigning queen is in this house. I've tried to allow him to grow and become a man. Make responsible decisions. After all, for now he is the only man in the house. He must accept that title with dignity and respect, for himself and this house, because when all else is said and done, I'm still the mama. Lord,

I hope this doesn't drive him to rebellion. I just want him to realize the seriousness of his actions and the choices he makes. If he doesn't follow simple rules around the house, Father, that black child is gone be in a world of trouble. It's already hard enough if you're a young black male and you're doing the right thing. What can I do? I don't know, just plant the best seed I can and pray it blossoms. In the meantime, hold him accountable for his actions and show the consequences. I do believe I did the right thing. Then why do I feel so bad? It just hurts to know he's behaving in such a way that I had to resort to such measures. We'll have to have another one of our talks. I'll try for it when he gets in from school tomorrow.

Until It's All Over

Tyler got out of second-period class and was headed to the quad area for nutrition when Mr. Jamerson, his math teacher, came up and spoke to him. "Hey, Tyler. How's it going?"

"Good," Tyler responded.

"How's basketball? I haven't been able to catch any of the games yet."

"Fine, we're four and zero."

"That's good. And what about your mom? She hasn't visited our campus lately. How is she?" Mr. Jamerson asked.

"She's fine. Been tripping lately though. But other than that, I guess she's all right." At the very moment Tyler spoke, he looked at Mr. Jamerson and thought to himself that he had gotten a good idea.

"Well, that's good. I think." Mr. Jamerson chuckled.

"Hey, Mr. Jamerson, I've checked out how you look at my mom when she comes up here. Why don't you ask her out?" Tyler suggested flatly.

"Hold up. Where did that come from? What do you mean the way I look at your mother?" Mr. Jamerson asked, surprised and agitated.

"Man, you know what I mean. And maybe if she had a boyfriend or something, she'd get off my back. Ask her out," Tyler explained.

Mr. Jamerson laughed. "And you think that will get her off your back? Let me tell you something Tyler. It's true your mother is a good-looking woman. She's not single because no one is interested in her or she can't get a date, and she's not on your case because she's lonely. She stays in your butt because she loves you and is concerned with you and your future. How many parents do you see around here visiting their kids' classes? Don't you realize she has to make time and effort to do that? Why? Because she cares. Because you would be buck wild if she didn't. She's on your case because *you* need it. If you did what you were supposed to do and what you're capable of doing, she wouldn't have to babysit you. But you better be glad she does 'cause things could be a whole lot worse. Look how spoiled you are. Walking around here in all the latest fashions, always clean and big as you are, even well-fed. Everybody doesn't have it like that. I bet all she asks is you handle your school duties and obey some funky little rules. And to show your respect and appreciation, you try to sick some man on her. You're the one tripping! You need to check yourself. You'll be grown soon, so you better be careful what you ask for. You just might get it."

"There you go lecturing. Never mind, man," Tyler said as he walked away.

"All right, Tyler. You better think about it. See you around," Mr. Jamerson called out behind him.

Tyler was about to go to the student store when the bell rang for third-period class to begin. He kicked his foot in disgust, realizing he wasted his entire nutrition time listening to Mr. Jamerson. He tried not to think about the words Mr. Jamerson spoke. They sounded too much like the words he heard from his mother. She must have said something to him during one of her spy visits. Tyler continued to class trying to pretend he didn't hear any of *their* words.

When Tyler came in from basketball practice, Chan had already prepared dinner and had an outline of the points she wanted to discuss with Tyler. Chan let Tyler eat, wind down, and get comfortable. Chan later cleared the dining table and went to her room to retrieve her checklist.

On her way back to the dining room, she stepped into the den and clicked off the TV.

"Tyler, I need to see you in the dining room," Chan said matter-of-factly.

Tyler immediately picked up on the tone in his mother's voice. He knew another discussion on life was in the making. Tyler dreaded these talks, but he knew one would soon be coming after their last episode. Fortunately, a lot of good always became of their talks also. He never really let in on it, but he appreciated the candid conversations his mom would have with him. She usually opened up and told a lot about herself as well as give him insight on life and the trials teenagers may encounter. He regularly thinks about the one they had when he turned thirteen and Chan thought a direct conversation about sex and drugs was in order.

He'll never forget the sigh of relief on his mother's face after she slid in the question about whether or not he was sexually active. When Tyler responded no, Chan tried to continue talking as if that wasn't necessarily the response she wanted to hear but was more interested in educating him. Tyler never hinted or revealed he could read how nervous his mom was at that moment. He was relieved the opportunity for communication was opened. As various events happened in the course of his teen years, some seemed to relate to the conversations with his mom, and somehow, they weren't so difficult to handle. He understands he doesn't have to learn everything from personal experience. The experience of others is sometimes lesson enough. This is why Tyler gets so frustrated when Chan gets on his case. He doesn't use drugs. He's not having sex, dealing drugs, ditching school, hanging out late, or running with gangs. What more could she possible want?

Chan must have known exactly what Tyler was thinking. After all, he is her son. The conversation opened up with a response to Tyler's very question.

"Son, there was a time when getting good grades was a parent's biggest worry or battle with their child. Nowadays, kids are faced with so many other adversities and distractions that can destroy them and their future. I've been blessed that you have not taken those paths. I am immeasurably grateful and proud of you, and I don't want you to ever think I'm not aware and appreciative of those accomplishments. The point I'm trying to make is in addition to staying away from the negative, you have to indulge in some positive. School and grades are important. None of those things are optional. I cannot and I will not sit back quietly and watch you fail. I have a minimum of eighteen years to teach, guide, and nurture you. You have maximum of eighteen years to take full advantage of my commitment. I don't make demands of you just because I have that authority. It's the best way *I* know to raise a man, to make a productive person out of you. I'm sure it's not the only way, maybe not even the right way, but it's my best. We can always talk about other options, but you must remember that getting your way, or doing things your way, has to be earned. The more responsibly you act, the more responsibilities you get. Understand that doing what you want, how you want, is indeed taking on a responsibility. It's being responsible enough to handle the new freedom, handle chosen tasks. Staying up late, going out with your friends, having a phone, watching TV and playing video games aren't your rights, they're privileges, and you *must* earn them."

The conversation took the path their conversations usually take. Chan does all the talking, and Tyler grunts, nods, stares into space, and sometimes responds if there's a direct question requiring an answer. Chan started talking again. "I'm not trying to make life difficult for you nor will I ever take any mess off you. Don't dare challenge me again. Please, son, don't make me hurt my only child." Chan attempted to soften the mood. "Try to understand my position. Whether you know it or not, I try hard as hell to understand your situation. Okay?"

Finally, Tyler spoke. "Okay."

Although he sat like a bump on a log, Tyler was listening to his mother. He didn't know how to let her know. He had been thinking himself since their incident, especially after that episode with Mr. Jamerson. He took out some time to review his relationship with his mom and all her efforts and sacrifices.

Tyler realized anyone devoted to someone as much as his mom is to him could only have their best interest in mind. Chan has been visiting schools; paying for tutoring, uniforms, and equipment; helping with homework; and supporting school activities for as long as he could remember. But he never really thought about it before now. She has also been driving back and forth to practices and events of every sport he's played and provided transportation to many of his friends and teammates. Chan has attended practically all his games and cheered relentlessly. Tyler thought about his mom in the stands during his game just the other day.

"All right, Stentorians. Let's go!" Chan shouted.

"Defense, defense, defense," the crowd chanted.

"Get in his face, Darnell!" Chan called out. She knew just about every player on the team. Those she didn't know knew her somehow. If nothing else, they knew she was Tyler's mom. That's Chan's life story. Always someone's, somebody—Clarice's daughter, Alisa's sister, Colby's partner, Tyler's mother. "Watch the lane!" Chan hollered out. The other team scored, and the Stentorian crowd quieted. "Come on now, Stentorians! Pick your man up. Close up the gap. Keep 'em out of the paint."

The Stentorians took the ball out under the basket and passed it to the point guard. Marcus started dribbling down court. Two defensive men picked him up at half-court. Marcus dribbled to the left, and Darnell gave him a screen. One defender pursued the ball, and Marcus did a crossover and reversed to the right, leaving the defender shaken out of his shoes. When another defender switched over to Marcus to pick up the slack, Marcus saw Tyler open. Marcus turned to the right and sent a no-look, powerful pass straight to Tyler who was breaking under the basket. Chan saw the move in the making.

When the ball reached Tyler's hands, Chan jumped straight up. She knew what was about to happen. Tyler caught the ball midair, gripped it, transferred it to his strong hand, palmed it, and sprung to the basket. Tyler soared to the hoop, body leaning and slam-dunked with the greatest of authority. The crowd oohed and stood to their feet to cheer.

"That's what I'm talking about! You go ahead and play basketball, son!" Chan shouted.

Several people in the crowd caught wind of Chan's comment and turned, smiling, to look at the source of that remark. Some simply chuckled in agreement; others responded.

"I know that's right," one gentlemen said.

"You tell 'em, girl," another voice from above suggested.

"Okay!" one other parent said as she reached up to give Chan a high five.

"Number 99 is your son?" the couple behind Chan leaned over to ask.

"Yes," Chan turned back to respond as she clapped the Stentorians on.

"He's good," the wife said.

"Thank you," Chan smiled.

As they all began to sit back down, Arnus stole the ball from the other team's point guard.

"All right now, Arnus. Run with it, Stentorians. Show them whose house this is!" Chan began to cheer again.

Arnus went for the fast break. He saw the lane open and tried to penetrate to the basket. As Arnus went up with the ball, his defender pounded him from behind. The referee gestured clean block by clapping his hands together.

Arnus looked at the referee as if to say, "What game are you watching?"

"Come on now, ref. You know that was a foul. Don't punish our kids 'cause they're good. You gonna cause an injury out there, letting that kinda stuff go unchecked!" Chan screamed.

Other fans were shouting similar comments, and the crowd began to boo. "Boo!" everyone shouted in unison.

At the very same moment, both teams were in the paint, scrambling for the ball. It went between the legs of one of the other team members, number 22. Tyler came up with the ball and laid it in gently. The crowd roared once again. They knew the Stentorians were fired up and was getting ready to get loose and run away with the game. Once again, the Stentorians ran all over their opposition. They won 93 to 51 and gave their supporters a good show.

After the game, Chan stayed seated in the stands, waiting for the crowed to disperse and Tyler to change out of his uniform. Everyone congratulated the players and the coach and shook their hands as they filed out of the gym, chattering about the Stentorians. As the players headed to the locker room, they saw Chan in the bleachers.

"Hi, Mom," Tyler said.

"Hi," Marcus called as he ran by.

"Hi, Ms. Tyler." Arnus smiled.

Jason, Tyler's best friend who plays football, ran over and sat down real quick and close to Chan, giving her a hug, and said, "Hi, Mom," playfully.

"How you doing, Jason?" Chan asked, laughing and enjoying the love from the big ole burly kids.

Jason jumped up as quickly as he had sat down and ran into the locker room to hang with Tyler and the rest of them. The others waved as they ran by the bleachers.

"How you doing, Ms. Blackmon?" the coach asked as he shook her hand.

"Fine. Thank you, Coach Horry," Chan responded. "Good game."

As Tyler thought about the enjoyment his mom had while cheering for him at his games, he smiled a little. He had to admit, he did enjoy her being there and showing her support. And everyone likes his mom. Tyler's thoughts were floating all over the place.

He sat at the dining room table, leaning over the side of his chair. He looked to have about as much interest in what Chan was saying as America has in helping out with the issues of Rwanda, and Haiti. Tyler was not yet ready to give in to this battle. He suppressed the growing realization that his mother was making sense. He still felt the urge to fight. How can she know everything? He was becoming a man. He needed more space, more freedom. So what she did all those things for him? She was supposed to; that's her job. She still didn't understand him. This was his life. He could do what he wanted to do.

"Mom, I'm tired of you treating me like a baby. I'm a man. I can do what I wanna do," Tyler argued.

Chan was surprised. Tyler never argued with her, especially not with such venom and intent. He usually sat there waiting for her to finish. She had to catch herself. She almost got furious. Then she thought, *Maybe this is good.* Finally, they would have some dialogue. Their conversation would be more than just her talking and then ending with her wondering if anything she said made sense to Tyler. If she got through to Tyler at all.

"Son, there will never be a time in your life when you can do whatever you want, whenever you want. All decisions and opportunities depend on other factors. Being a man includes handling responsibility. Age alone does not dictate manliness or adulthood," Chan responded.

"I am responsible," Tyler announced.

"In what way? Tell me what it is you do or have done that would deem this conversation unnecessary?" Chan inquired.

"I go to school, I take out the trash, I wash dishes, I clean the house," Tyler listed.

"Yeah, and you do it because you have no choice, not because you're acting responsible and taking care of business. And even those routine drills require constant prompting and nagging. What do you do on you own that would show maturity? Your grades certainly aren't reflecting any signs of a responsible person."

Tyler was stumped. He hadn't thought this whole scenario through before he engaged in this verbal challenge with his mother. She also caught him off guard when she calmly replied to his outburst. He was fully prepared to start ducking and dodging fist and even storm out the house if he had to. How would she like that? That would show her he's not playing; that he means business.

"What would you do if I just left? Right now," Tyler threatened.

"I'd get in your case for walking away from me while I'm talking to you. I'd point out the immaturity of that gesture and ask what form of responsibility you're displaying with that act. Ultimately, I'd remind you that you have a curfew, and you aren't running nothing around here but your mouth. And if you aren't more selective on how you use it, you're gonna get popped right in it," Chan answered.

There it was. The invitation to a duel Tyler had been looking for. Tyler tried to plant the seed that if Chan ran him away, there was no telling what could happen to him. Consequently, it would be best to leave him alone to do what he wanted so she wouldn't be subjected to that worry or burden.

"What would you do if I left and something happened to me?" Tyler asked.

Chan spoke softly and decisively. "Tyler, you're my son and I love you deeply, and because of that, I can't watch you self-destruct without making some attempt to intervene and redirect your path. If something terrible happened to you because you blatantly disregarded all I've taught you and all the rules around the house, I'd do two things for certain. I'd pray for your soul and peace in my life to understand that I did the best I could. How much would I miss you? I can't imagine nor do I think words exist for an adequate explanation of the hole that would replace my heart. What frightens me is you don't understand right now how much you're tearing my heart apart, acting and talking this way. I'm going to bed now."

Chan was opening her journal to put in her daily entry. Well, the entries weren't so daily lately. They were far more few and in between and were usually stemmed from an event that was deemed to be immortalized. This entire day had somehow made itself noteworthy, especially that run-in with her ex-boyfriend, Marcus. He caught sight of Chan and cursed her up one side and down the other. She was definitely compelled to jot down that theatrical scene.

While flipping through the pages to get to the next blank sheet, she ran across an entry that confirmed her suspicions of being an asshole magnet.

*01/28*

Today, I had a date, or what was supposed to be a date. I met this guy at the grocery store a couple of weeks ago. He seemed nice; had a bright smile and an okay conversation from what I could judge in such surroundings and limited time. We spoke on the phone several times prior to this so-called date, and things went smoothly. There were no hints of jerk/asshole slipping into the conversation. The creep monitor didn't go off. (I've got to replace the batteries on that thing!) So we planned a date to catch a movie or dinner and see how things would work out. Well, we apparently have two very different interpretations of "see how things work out." I let Tyler spend the night at a friend's so he wouldn't be home alone and would not be subjected to meeting the gentleman or any other gentlemen picking me up until I knew them a lot better.

Mr. What's His Name gets here and wants to watch the rest of the game. In an effort to be reasonable, I don't trip and offer him a wine cooler in the meantime. At the end of the game, without any prompting, he decides we're going to stay here and make out. Psycho! I asked him what time the show starts and shouldn't we get going. He tells me the wine cooler got him a little tipsy, and he didn't think he should drive. Right! I see where this is going. He was trying to get a little too comfortable. So I offered to drive. Um, here comes excuse number two. He gives this story about having a long day and getting tired and possibly falling asleep at the movies. Then he tells me to come over and sit by him and talk to him. Tell him more about myself.

Oh boy, here we go. His hands got to roaming. He was trying to neck, in a failing attempt to turn me on. Ugh, I had to get out of that one. I excused myself to the bathroom, and I picked up my phone on the way. I called Tamara to have her call me back with an emergency. Any emergency. That fool called back talking about she had a booger stuck in her hair, and she really needed help. (How was I supposed to keep a straight face with that sort of an emergency? But I did.) I took the call and got the hell out of there (running from my own home, that's crazy) and took my damn self to the movies. I hope he got the hint and never calls back again. Is it me, or is he such a creep that he would treat all women like that? Sad thing is he's not the first one and may not be the last. How disheartening.

Until Tomorrow

After reading that excerpt, Chan giggled at the thought of the experiences she's had in her years of dating. Luckily, she was able to find some amusement in it all. Otherwise, the view would be very dismal.

Although she didn't believe the hype about having no good brothers available, the encounters and experiences of relationships to this point were pretty grim. She held on to the belief and hope that the right one hadn't come along, and she would not force the wrong one to fit. She only prayed she would not be tainted when he did come along. This latest event was certainly one that could place a blemish on her view of the relationship market.

06/14

Today, there was a Marcus sighting. I don't know if I willed this to happen or if I simply knew strongly of the probability of it happening, which is why I broke it off in the first place. That man saw me and lost his entire mind. He cursed me up one side and down the other. Told me how *good* I think I am (no, it's how good *you* think I am) and how my pussy bleeds just like all the other whores. Now I'm not sure if that gut stab meant I was a whore in particularly or that all women are alike in his eyes. He was correct on one issue. I certainly do bleed, on a regular basis, like the majority of us, whores, lesbians, virgins, or otherwise.

Anyway, he certainly cleared up any confusion or regrets I may have had about acting hastily on ending the relationship. He managed to recreate every image in my mind that led me to terminate the relationship and all the images that told me I should have gotten out sooner. And who was he calling a whore? He was the womanizing, tail-chasing freak disguised as a gentleman.

Nonetheless, it was interesting. Hopefully, he got it all off his chest, and we won't have any more of those moments again. I can be less nervous when I'm in places he may also visit. The initial shock and surprise factor is over.

Until Tomorrow

# Marriage

Max was sitting in her living room, staring into space, thinking about Kelly. She was moved by Kelly's strength. She knew Kelly was brilliant and tenacious, but she would have never expected she would ever have to face a trial of this magnitude. She thought, *But this attitude is actually characteristic of Kelly. She is wimpy and frantic on small issues—that's the drama in her—and a Rock of Gibraltar when you least expect it, on issues that would incapacitate the average person.*

Although Kelly seemed to take this challenge with a positive outlook, Max couldn't bring herself to tell Kelly about her pregnancy. It saddened her to think her life was going so well, all things considered, and her bestest—yes, bestest—friend was experiencing the trial of a lifetime. And Max couldn't do anything about it. Max and Tony agreed to keep the pregnancy a secret, but Max knew she probably would have told Kelly under better circumstances.

Somehow, Max didn't find it fair to have good news, knowing Kelly's predicament. Max sat there reviewing the day in her head, replaying the scenarios, reliving the laughter, and trying to come up with some sort of balance to all the recent events.

When the phone rang, it startled Max. She jumped and looked around, searching for her phone. She just had it moments ago when Tony called to tell her he would be late. The phone was on its third ring, and Max was getting flustered. It would go to voicemail soon. She had to run all the way upstairs to find it. Just as Max found the phone in their bedroom, she grabbed it. "Hello?" she answered in a pant.

"Hey, girl. Catch you at a bad time?" Josh asked, chuckling.

"Shut up, turkey." Max collapsed across the bed. "I had to run upstairs to catch the phone. I didn't know what the heck I did with this thing. I just had it. My phone gets lost more than the remote control. Anyway, what's up? How are you doing?"

"I'm good. What about you?"

"Fine. Just fine," Max responded.

"You sure? You're never fine, just fine. You sound distant. You sure I haven't caught you at a bad time?" Josh asked again.

"Yeah, I'm sure," Max said with certainty.

"All right then. How's Tony doing?" Josh said.

"He's good, thank you."

"Girl, you're up to something, but I won't sweat you. Called to run a little something by you."

"What's up?" Max inquired.

"I'm gonna ask Kelly to marry me," Josh blurted out.

A chill ran up Max's spine. She knew Josh had always been crazy about Kelly, but where did this come from? They weren't even seeing one another. She secretly hoped

Kelly and Josh would get together, but now things were different. Max tried to figure out how she should respond to Josh. How did he expect her to respond? How could she respond? *Does he know? Should I tell him?* Max thought.

"I was just sitting here thinking about Kelly," Max said casually.

"Max, you're a trip. I just dropped life-changing, prodigious news on you, and you take it all cool and carefree. Like you'd been waiting on this call all day."

"Yeah, just when I thought nothing else could shock me," Max murmured under her breathe.

"What was that?" Josh asked.

"Did I say that out loud? Oh, nothing."

"So why were you thinking about Kelly?" Josh asked.

"I don't know. She just came to mind, and I started daydreaming, reminiscing."

"Oh. So what do you think about what I just said? You're acting all basic, like you don't want to hear what I'm saying."

"No, no, no. That's not it at all, Josh. I'm trying to grasp all this, make some sense out of it. Put it together 'cause I apparently missed something. You know this is a serious surprise."

"So that's why you're acting all stank?"

"Dang, Josh, I'm sorry. I mean, what am I supposes to say? You call with this staggering news, and I'm trying to figure out when this happened. You know? When did you guys date? When did you fall in love? All I know now is you want to get married, and I don't know where it's coming from. You're just gonna ask Kelly to marry you out of the blue, or what's going on?"

"Max, you know I've been after Kelly for a long time now. I think I've been in love with her since I first met her. She simply would not give me any play. I guess she didn't take me seriously," Josh explained.

"What makes you think she will give you any play now?" Max asked.

"She already has," Josh responded proudly.

Max gasped. "You and Kelly been fucking?" Max asked sarcastically but with the intention of getting the juicy news. In the immediate moment to follow, the gasp of delight quickly shifted to fear upon the realization of the end result of their intimacy.

"Now, Miss Max, it's not cool to be all up in folks' business," Josh chastised teasingly.

"I was just playing. But on the serious side, you guys been sneaking around for a while, huh? Are you sure this is what you want to do?" Max's tone changed.

"I've never been more certain about anything in my life," Josh responded with an even more serious tone.

"Have you and Kelly talked about it?"

"No, she will probably be just as shocked as you were."

"Josh, I think you should have a good talk with Kelly. There are some things you guys should discuss," Max vaguely warned.

"Max, I was there just before you came by Kelly's place Saturday. I know what she wanted to discuss with you, and I was also there after you dropped her off."

"Ohhh, that was you? So you know everything? Man, why didn't you lead with that important bit of information? Got me over here dancing on egg shells and stumbling all over the place!"

"I'm sorry. I didn't know she didn't tell you about us," Josh apologized.

"So you've really thought about what you might be getting into? You aren't doing this out of pity or anything like that, are you?" Max inquired.

"No, hell nawl! I understand the life cycle of HIV. You know I lost two of my buddies to that shit. Out there getting with every skirt that crossed their paths. I saw the deterioration their bodies and mind experienced and the pain and heartache it caused. To them and their families. I know you can't play with someone's feelings, and pity won't get me through the struggle should this illness begin to consume Kelly. But I believe my love will."

"Okay, okay. I didn't want to have to jack you up for messing over my friend, man," Max warned and teased. "So you're absolutely sure this is what you want to do?" Max asked again.

Josh responded, "110 percent."

"How long you guys been going out?"

"Oh, Lord. Here comes twenty questions. About eight months."

"Eight months! And you two been keeping it a secret all this time? Oooh, I'm gonna hurt somebody. So how did it start?"

"Actually, I was sort of leaning on her after ole girl dismissed me. Although I didn't really care about the breakup,

I was wondering if I was really an asshole and would end up by myself forever or what. We started having deep conversations, real conversations, and it just got better with time."

"And how long have you known?" Max asked.

"Almost immediately. She tried to use it to push me away. In retrospect, I think that's why she kept me at a distance. Well, that and the fact that I wasn't coming correctly."

"Yeah, you weren't quite ready yet. So how did you get her to give you the time of day this time? Never mind. You did, and look what's happening. Oooh, now I'm excited. I'm very happy for both of you. I know there's a blessing in every crisis," Max encapsulated.

"Thanks, Max. That really makes me feel better, knowing we have your blessings. I was gonna ask her anyway, but I was hoping you'd be happy for us," Josh retorted.

"So when are you going to ask her?" Max asked.

"Sometime between now and Sunday. The ring will be ready Tuesday."

"Ooooh, I wanna see," Max whined.

"Not before Kelly," Josh scorned.

"Okay! So how are you going to ask her? What are you going to do?" Max quizzed with excitement.

"I don't know yet. It'll be quiet. You know Kelly doesn't like a whole lot of drama," Josh responded.

"All women like drama when it comes to marriage. You're just chicken. You don't want to be embarrassed if she says *no*!" Max teased.

"Well, that too. I know Kelly will try to make excuses and change my mind because of her situation. Under the current circumstances, I think it might be best if I did a little romantic dinner and evening and ask her sometime during the night."

"Maybe you're right. So you're gonna ask at dinner?" Max tried to confirm.

"Damn, Columbo! Is this an investigation? You know, you're nosy. I'm just messing with you, Max. I don't know. I'll play it by ear. When I feel my muse," Josh answered.

"Forget you, Josh. You make me sick. Gone with your ole stanky, secretive self. I don't even care. But you better call me when you get your answer," Max joked.

"Nope," Josh teased.

"Bye, Josh," Max hung up on him.

Josh laughed out loud on the other end of the line. He has always known how to get Max worked up. He called her right back.

"Hello?" Max answered.

"I don't believe you hung up on me," Josh hung up on her.

It was Max's turn to laugh. She laughed and shook her head. Max put the phone back down and smiled as she walked downstairs.

Shortly after Josh hung up with Max, he called Kelly to arrange a date for the big question. Josh recently heard about a play coming to town, opening Thursday night. The title *When Love Calls* caught his attention. He thought it might be interesting. That would be the perfect excuse to get Kelly out. If the play was anything like the title, maybe it would help him out a little. Kinda set the mood.

"Kelly, what's on your agenda Thursday?" Josh asked.

"Thursday lunch or evening?" Kelly asked.

"Thursday evening."

"Nothing really. What's up?"

"There's a play starting Thursday. I was thinking we should go."

"Oh yeah, *When Love Calls*. I want to see that too. I heard about it on the radio the other day. Okay," Kelly agreed.

"Cool. I'll pick up some tickets tomorrow and let you know what time it starts. Maybe we can go to dinner before the play," Josh suggested.

"That'll work," Kelly agreed.

"So what you up to?" Josh asked.

"Not much. Sitting here, thinking about you."

"Oh really? What you thinking about me?" Josh inquired playfully.

"I'm not telling," Kelly teased.

"Oh, it's like that, huh?"

"Yep, at least until you get here," Kelly replied suggestively.

"Is that right? I'll be right there, chief," Josh said in his best Maxwell Smart impression. "Have you eaten yet? You want me to bring something?"

Josh's phone clicked when Kelly answered him. "Yeah, I did. I picked up something on my way home. I didn't feel like cooking."

"Hold on a second, Kelly," Josh requested.

"Go ahead."

Josh needed to distance himself from Kelly until Thursday so he wouldn't let on to his plans. He hoped the absence would make the heart grow fonder. Except for one thing—he couldn't resist her. He enjoyed Kelly's company and longed for her touch whenever they were apart. And he certainly couldn't tell her *no*. Consequently, he was making plans to go to Kelly tonight and try to be strong again the next couple of days.

Now that he had made up his mind to give in, the call on the other line changed his mind again. It was his mother. She needed his help. Josh clicked back over to Kelly after a good minute.

"Sorry about that."

"That's okay."

"Bad news. That was my mom. Her faucet broke. I have to go pick up some parts and fix it for her. I can still come by when I finish, but it might be late," Josh explained.

"That's okay. I have some paperwork I should finish up anyway. I was being lazy and putting it off. Say hello to your mom for me."

"*You* were putting off work for me? Uh-oh, I'm getting to you," Josh teased as he ignored Kelly trying to be cool.

"Just tell your mom I said hi," Kelly laughed.

"Okay. If I get in too late, I'll call you tomorrow."

"All right, babe. Bye," Kelly closed.

"Goodnight, love," Josh hung up.

Josh made reservations at the Ritz Carlton restaurant in Buckhead, Georgia, and picked up the ring Tuesday after work. It was beautiful. A total of five carats with a three-carat pear-shaped solitaire that fit into a band surrounded by baguettes and round diamonds.

Josh was doing pretty good, keeping busy and staying away from Kelly. For a brief moment, Kelly wondered if Josh was trying to avoid her. Although they talked daily, usually several times a day, she hadn't seen him for a few days. He finagled himself out of a lunch date with her on Tuesday. She hated to think Josh was avoiding her, but she told herself she could understand his apprehension if indeed that is what he was doing. Her internal conversation tried to convince her she could deal with it. Of course, she could. She had to. How could she really expect someone to seriously take on a new relationship with someone who has AIDS? People in love and married for years break up over things like that or even smaller things, so she told herself she understood. Her mouth understood, maybe even her mind understood, but her heart did not understand.

The bare thought that Josh wanted out saddened Kelly. She was caught up. She gave into Josh, and he was as good to her as she was afraid he would be. Wonderful, like she expected of him because she has always known the kindness of Josh's heart. She was just afraid he would not be as ready as he thought he was.

Kelly decided to dismiss the negative thoughts and enjoy whatever they had and for however long it would last. Besides, there really was no reason for her to be tripping. When she and Josh first got together, she told him if things ever got too tough for him to handle, he could walk away without any guilt. She only asked that he let her know first and not diss her without any words. Kelly felt confident Josh was man enough and intelligent enough to express his thoughts.

It was killing Josh to stay away from Kelly the past few days. He knew she would know he was up to something. Since Josh lacked all skills in masquerading, he put Max up to entertaining Kelly until Thursday. He figured if she was sidetracked, she wouldn't notice his disappearance too much. Kelly did notice Josh was missing in action but would not make anything of it since they had a date Thursday. Now if he canceled or stood her up, then she'd have to rethink the latest events. Since Kelly hadn't told Max about Josh and her dating, she couldn't discuss the issue with her. Therefore, she had to find other things to focus on.

Josh was going crazy trying to figure out exactly how and when during the evening he would ask Kelly to marry him. He wanted to consult with Max, but he knew Miss Max would do entirely too much. She'd be camping out at the restaurant trying to see everything to make sure it went exactly according to her script. No, he didn't want that pressure.

Josh picked Kelly up at six o'clock for their seven-o'clock dinner reservations. Kelly left work a little early to get ready for their date. She bathed in her soap and oil set of smell good and spruced her hair up. She put on her Donna Karan ice-blue sheath dress with the split in front of the right thigh. She looked fabulous as usual. Kelly topped her outfit off with a pair of five-inch French blue nubuck sling-back pumps. They extended her long, lean legs and highly defined her thigh and calf muscles. Kelly hated wearing stockings and always debated the issue of wearing them. The choice to wear them usually only won for church, very special occasions, and cold weather. This time, stockings lost again. She thought her bare legs were sexy.

When Josh walked in, he took one look at Kelly and confirmed within himself another reason he was so crazy about her. What man could ask for more? Brains, beauty, can cook, and was very attractive in a relationship.

"Damn girl, let's just turn on some music, hang out here, and you sashay around those pumps and sleek-ass legs for me," Josh suggested.

"I don't think so, brotha. You promised me a date, and that's just what we're gonna do. I want my dinner, my play, some dancing, a late-night stroll, and breakfast at sunrise," Kelly rattled off.

"Whoa, whoa, whoa. Sounds like you're embellishing the itinerary. I said dinner and a play. Where'd all those extra events come from? Dancing? Breakfast? I don't think so, missy. One happy meal and one puppet show. That's it. Then back home and to bed for you, young lady. Josh teased.

"Ah, that's messed up, Josh. So that's your idea of a great night out?" Kelly responded playfully.

"That's right. I had to dip into my life savings for this kid's meal tonight, so you better enjoy it. We better get going before the drive thru gets too crowded."

Kelly approached Josh sensuously. "Did I tell you how good you look tonight?"

"Nope, as a matter of fact you didn't." Josh stepped back and posed, doing his best impression of a GQ model.

"Good, I was afraid I had relapsed and started lying again," Kelly laughed as she walked back up to hug Josh.

"It's like that now?" Josh asked, sweeping Kelly around her waist, pulling her close to him, and kissing her lips.

They went to eat first, and everything went well. They had a table in the center of the room on the north end of the restaurant—the section of the restaurant usually reserved for a special evening. The waitress was very attentive, and the food was excellent and plentiful.

This was Kelly's first visit to the Ritz. She was admiring everything. The atmosphere and décor were astonishing. It was so romantic and eloquent. The music was soothing, and the dimly lit chandeliers offered a nice touch to the serenity and romance of the place. Kelly was definitely feeling romantic. She and Josh talked and laughed, toasted, and enjoyed their dinner. During their toast, Kelly took notice of how deeply she was falling in love with Josh with each passing moment. *What a perfect love affair. Really good friends first, really good friends still, mutual respect, and common interests. Who'd have ever thought? Slow down, Kelly. Don't push. Just enjoy the moment. Don't expect too much.*

Josh was busy debating in his head as to whether or not this was the right moment. *If not now, when? And how? And what will I say? She can't say no. What if she says no? Lord, don't let her say no.*

While they were waiting for the waitress to return with the receipt, an orchestra version of a song Josh recognized floated through the room via piped-in ceiling speakers.

Josh stood and walked a couple of steps to Kelly's side. He held out his hand and bowed slightly.

"May I have this dance my lady?" Josh asked.

Kelly looked up at Josh astonished and slightly embarrassed. "Right now, Josh?" she whispered.

Josh said nothing. At the same time he was preparing to nod his head in order to inform Kelly "absolutely," something moved Kelly. No embarrassment or opinion of others could keep her from this moment. It was priceless. It was precious. It was perfect. It would have been unrecoverable. Kelly rose from her seat with the grace of an African princess. She wrapped her arms around Josh's neck and buried her head on his chest. Josh rested one of his hands in the small of Kelly's back and the other on the upper middle of her back. He held her close, gently. They remained in that position almost motionless. They were lost in each other's soul.

Josh no longer heard the sound of music. They never heard the song end. It was the claps of the waitress and the other patrons that woke them from their trance. Slightly embarrassed, they released one another and smiled and slightly bowed to their audience. Josh placed the tip on the table, Kelly grabbed her purse, and they left.

After they left the play, Josh took Kelly to their favorite dance spot on Peachtree Street. On their way to the club, they talked about the play and the scenes they liked or didn't particularly enjoy. They really enjoyed the play, and Kelly was having the best night of her life. The theater was the only place Kelly had actual knowledge regarding their voyages. Each stop was a lovely surprise. While they were riding, she asked no questions concerning their destinations. She just sat back and enjoyed the ride, the intrigue, and Josh's company. When they pulled up to the club, Josh parked and went around to open Kelly's door.

"How's this for your long list of date requirements, Miss Lady?"

In her best Southern belle accent, "Why, yes, Mr. Dawson, I do believe this meets my expectations."

"Well, prepare to get dazzled, my lady."

When Josh and Kelly walked into the club, the music was jumping and lively. Without any prompting or particular decision or awareness on their part, their heads began bobbing, and they sauntered to the sound of the beat. Josh grabbed Kelly's hand, and they headed straight to the dance floor. An hour passed before they came off the floor. Josh went to the bar to get them a drink, and Kelly stood around near the dance floor and an open door to get some air. There were no seats and very little standing room.

While Josh pushed through the crowd, he wondered when he would propose to Kelly. Time was running out, but there was nowhere to sit, no privacy, here. Should they leave? Should they stay? Should he get on his knees? Should he ask her here or during the stroll on the boardwalk at the park that he planned for them after they finished dancing?

Somewhere between the trip from the bar to Kelly, he made a decision. They stood around and danced and talked amongst themselves and to friends they ran across. A table came available, and they sat and finished their drinks. Moments later, they were back on the dance floor having big fun. Kelly and Josh were in the zone. All their dance moves were on; they fed off one another. As the night crept on, they continued to dance, resting only when absolutely necessary. They bopped, they hip-hopped, they "reggaed," they slow-danced, "cha-cha'd," and anything else they could do if the music called for it.

When the music commanded a swing/salsa/step/do-whatever-you-can-Josh thing, Josh slipped in a proposal. He and Kelly were dancing their hearts out. Their feet were going and Kelly's' hips were swaying and Josh was feverishly trying to keep up and remember the moves the girls had taught him. It seemed the crowd had taken particular interest in watching the performance of Josh and Kelly. Somewhere during one of those twirls and spin-outs of Kelly's, the DJ handed Josh a microphone as he had requested while making one of his runs to the bar. When Kelly spun back into Josh's arms, he spoke into the microphone.

"Miss Kelly LeBeau, will you marry me?"

Kelly stood there, still in Josh's arm, staring in his face. She translated the words for the third time, and they still kept coming back the same. Josh had asked her to marry him. Right here. In the middle of the dance floor. In front of all these people. He was really in rare form.

"Miss Kelly LeBeau, will you marry me?" Before Kelly responded, Josh released her and took a small step back. He took Kelly by her left hand, removed the ring from his pocket, and got down on one knee. "I would be honored if you would be my wife and my friend for the rest of my life."

The stunned crowd finally broke their silence as they admired the breathtaking ring Josh offered Kelly. The ladies aahed at the words Josh had spoken. Kelly finally spoke.

"Yes, yes, Josh. I would love to be your wife and everything to you that you are to me!" Tears began to well in her eyes.

Josh placed the engagement ring on Kelly's finger, stood up, and hugged his fiancée. The crowd applauded and congratulated them. The women hugged Kelly and whispered words of encouragement and accolades for the fine catch she'd made. Josh is fine and apparently thoughtful. The brothas gave Josh dap and embraces separated by their forearm and hands entwined as their chest bumped. Many offered their approval of his choice in women and to settle down. Others offered their condolences in jest for being taken out of the "free and single circuit" and cashing in his playa' tokens. The DJ announced the next song he was playing was for the happy couple. The dance floor opened up, and they danced cheek to cheek for the entire song. The rest of the partygoers joined them as the DJ mixed in the next love song. Kelly and Josh were celebrities in their own right for the remainder of the evening until they left.

It was not yet time for the night to end. They slipped out of the club shortly before closing, and Josh drove to the boardwalk. They got out of the car and walked amongst the stars and the city lights. They were oblivious to the people around them, just as the other couples were oblivious to them.

Kelly was in ecstasy. This was, by far, the absolute most wonderful night of her life. The fairy tale she once envisioned that was shattered and believed to be an impossible dream had now come true. Josh loved her just as much as she tried not to love him. He was so wonderful. Everything she hoped for. She wanted the night to never end. She wanted to hold on to the feeling for as long as she could. At least until tomorrow. But she knew she couldn't wait too long before she told Josh she couldn't marry him.

Although Kelly deeply loves Josh and she believes he loves her sincerely enough, she can't help but think he's asking her to marry him out of pity, sympathy, and obligation. That had to be it. Why else would he want to marry someone in her condition? She wouldn't be around long enough to make him happy. All their memories will be of her illness, and their married days will be of him taking care of her. Josh is a good man, and she felt he deserved better than a life doomed to nursing her and waiting on death. Kelly decided she'd talk to Josh Sunday evening so they could discuss it before anyone else found out about the proposal.

When Josh came over, Kelly greeted him with her usual sweetness and got straight to the point.

"Josh, you don't have to do this," Kelly suggested.

"Do what? What are you talking about Kelly?"

"Marriage. You don't have to do this. You aren't obligated to spend the rest of my life with me. I don't want to burden you with my illness. Things are fine just as they are. You deserve a better life than what I can offer."

"Oh, there it is. I fooled myself into believing I was out of the woods after you accepted my proposal and the weekend was going so well. I fully expected you to try and get out of the engagement sooner, but I guess it was bound to happen. Well, let me tell you something woman. I don't need your approval on what I want to do with my life. Granted, I have to have your approval to marry you, but all this crap about obligation, burden, and what I deserve… You can save that drama. Don't you think I thought about this before I made any decisions? Give me some sort of credit for common sense. I know what I'm getting into. I watched not one but two of my closest buddies die from complications related to AIDS. I understand the concept of unconditional love. You aren't the only one capable of researching and analyzing. I realize the work involved in dealing with this illness. What you don't realize is I don't have a choice in this matter. My life will forever have a deep void if I don't share every available and precious moment I can with you as my wife. So if you're telling me no, don't do it on the premise of my well-being. Do it because you don't love me the way I love you. Do it because you don't want to spend the rest of our lives together."

Kelly was speechless. She didn't expect Josh to go off on her. She thought she had prepared a response for all his arguments. Wrong. She was particularly thrilled to hear his love ran so deep that there was not even a hint of compunction in his proposal. Kelly had no rebuttal; the only words she could muster up was truth.

"I do love you the same," she murmured, ashamed she had ever doubted Josh.

"I know you do. So stop tripping and pick a date," Josh chastised.

# Truth

MAX FINALLY GOT AROUND TO talking to Chan and Dede about Kelly. Chan took the news about as Max had expected. She only asked questions about Kelly's well-being and showed interest in determining how they could help. She asked no questions regarding how she may have contracted the disease or any of the down-low surrounding the situation. Her greatest emotional battle was with the revelation that it was full-blown AIDS and not the virus. She realized despite your intellect and any knowledge you may have on the subject, you still expect to *see* AIDS on a person, and that just isn't the case until the disease is challenged by an outside illness and it monopolizes the body. But, if your body isn't responsive to the meds, it's equally as damaging, infectious, and deadly leading up to the time you're visibly ill. After they finished discussing various points on the issue, Chan asked the infamous question. Their response to all occasions—happy, sad, mad, depressed, jazzed, sick, or elated.

"So when are we going shopping?"

"I know that's right." Max laughed. "We'll all need to get together soon and do that. Now I gotta call Dede."

Max wasn't too enthusiastic about calling Dede. She knew how dramatic Dede could be. She didn't know what response to expect out of her. She wasn't sure she could handle Dede's hysteria over the phone. Max took in a deep breath and picked up the phone to call her. In one way, Max was hoping Dede wasn't in, and on the other hand, she wanted to get this particular conversation over. Regardless of the tangent it might take. The phone was on its fourth ring. Max found herself subconsciously praying Dede would not answer. She began formulating the message she would leave on Dede's voicemail. The phone rang two more times, and Max started wondering what was taking Dede's phone so long to go to voicemail.

"Hello?" Dede answered.

"Dede?" Max asked, surprised to hear a voice.

"Who were you expecting, goofy?" Dede questioned.

"Actually, no one. The phone rang so many times that I was waiting on your voicemail."

"Oh, I was on the other line. I was trying to get off the phone but took a minute. So what's up?"

"I'm calling to pass on some information. I don't particularly like the assignment, but I did promise I would do it," Max explained.

"What assignment? What information?"

"I promised Kelly I would let the rest of us know."

"Know what?" Dede asked, exasperated. "Stop talking in riddles."

"That Kelly has AIDS," Max said solemnly.

"She has what! Kelly who? Our Kelly?" Dede grilled, obviously becoming upset.

"You heard me right. Yes, our Kelly. She recently told me and wanted you guys to know but didn't want to keep telling this story."

"But wait a minute, Max. You mean HIV, right? When did this happen? She can't possibly have AIDS just like that."

"No, I mean AIDS. She has full-blown AIDS, and it obviously happened some years ago."

"Oh my God. Has she known the whole time? Is she okay? When did you find out? Why is she just now telling us?"

"Calm down, Dede. No, she didn't know the whole time actually. She recently found out about a year or so ago, and she told me about a week ago. Right now she's doing okay. But she's not sure how things will continue to go, so she wanted us to know. You know it's tough holding on to something like that."

"Yeah, that's true. I feel awful for her. So what are we going to do?"

"Nothing. I mean, nothing different. Right now everything is still okay. She doesn't want us to act differently. Just continue to love and support her."

"Oh, no doubt. She's in my prayers. When are we getting together again? Does Chan and Josh know?"

"Yep. I just told Chan, and Josh knew before me. He was the very first person she told. They're together. In fact, they're getting married." At the very moment Max said those words, she wanted to take them back. Not that there was anything wrong with Dede knowing, but it dawned on her Kelly might want to tell them.

"What? They're getting married? Wait a minute. When did this happen? When did they even get together? With every passing sentence, you drop another bombshell. Does he know what he's getting himself into? Why would he do something like that? I don't get it. Why would anyone go into a situation like that, prewarned? Doesn't he think he's worthy of a life better than that?"

"Whoa, whoa. Excuse me?" Max went from zero to incensed in 0.0 seconds. "Worthy of better? Are you out of your damned mind? You can't get any better than Kelly! What the hell just happened here? A second ago you were loving Kelly, feeling her pain, having her back, and now you don't think she's good enough for someone? You need to check yourself and that bullshit at the door."

"No, you know what I mean. You know. She's gonna die. He's setting himself up for pain and disaster."

"We're all gonna die! But it's not about that. It's about celebrating life. He's setting himself up for happiness. You know like I know he's been in love with Kelly forever. You are tripping. I don't even believe you. See, that's your problem. Always trying to be man-worthy. And where has your perfection gotten you? Mixed up with a bunch of fools. Men who think you're a trophy and your ass acting like a trophy. Still you're alone. At least she has someone who loves her unconditionally," Max preached.

"Max, I wasn't saying that. You didn't have to be so mean."

"Apparently, I did. You talking all that insanity. You know what? I'm gonna talk to you later. Much later. Maybe you should rethink your group of friends. We can only deal with groovy people," Max cut at Dede.

Dede tried to snap back and defend herself. "You know, you're taking this too far and way out of context, as usual. Whenever someone doesn't share your exact views on an issue, you dismiss them. Go off and put them out of your world. Well, it ain't always about you and how you see things. Your perspective ain't gospel! Who christened you Mother Teresa?"

"Are you quite finished?"

"Maybe," Dede responded, trying to sustain her strength.

Max hung up the phone. She didn't feel she had to listen to Dede and her ignorant views. She knew there was a reason she was hesitant to call Dede. For all she cared, Dede could get on with that madness. There was no way she would let Dede bring Kelly down with that kind of attitude. She couldn't wait to call Chan and tell her what that fool Dede said. She called Chan's number and it went straight to voicemail. She knew Chan normally takes her calls, so she called her right back. Chan answered the phone. "Hello?"

"Hey, I just called. It went straight to voicemail," Max started.

"Really? It just rang a second ago when Dede called. Maybe that's why. You guys must have been calling at the same time."

"Oh, she called you?" Max asked with attitude.

"Yeah, she's on the other line. Let me call you right back."

"Make sure you do. I don't believe she called you."

"Why? What happened? Never mind, I'll call you back." Chan clicked the phone and was back on the line with Dede.

"That was Max, wasn't it?" Dede asked.

"Yeah. What's up with you two?"

"She called to tell me about Kelly and then she told me Kelly and Josh are getting married and...," Dede started explaining.

"Really? They're getting married?"

"See, it surprised you too. Except my response wasn't quite as positive. I sort of wondered out loud why. She took it for me saying Kelly wasn't worthy of him marrying her."

"You said what?"

"Don't go there, Chan. I just wondered if Josh was truly aware of what he was getting into. You know, in my field, I see too many people get destroyed by AIDS—the ones with the disease and the ones who tried to endure the struggle with their loved ones. Many can't hang, and the patient ends up alone, depressed and dying."

"Well, you know we would never let Kelly be alone. Even if Josh wasn't marrying Kelly, he would stick around as the valued friend we all are."

"I know that. That's why I feel so bad that my initial reaction came out my mouth. I was speaking more in general than of their personal situation. The surprise of the subject made me think about the changes people in the industry go through, and Max was not trying to hear me at all after that. She went dead off and hung up in my face."

"You know how extreme Max can be. Just give her a minute. She'll be all right. I'll talk to her," Chan suggested.

"You know I love Kelly just as much as the rest of you guys. I'm sad and happy for her, and I don't want this drama on top of anything else she has to deal with."

"I know you do, girl. Don't trip. This will get squashed real quick, and we'll all get together and have some fun."

"Make sure you let me know when," Dede warned.

"I will. Don't worry about Max. You know how over-protective she is. She would have gone smooth off on me if I said something wrong about you. She'll come around. I'll talk to you later, okay?"

"Okay," Dede agreed, reluctant to let go and hang up.

Dede feared if she hung up the phone, that would be her last ties with her friends. She thought Max would convince Chan to also turn against her.

Chan called Max back. Before Max could start her story, Chan took a bite out of Max's head. "You didn't tell me Josh and Kelly are getting married!" Chan hollered.

"I know, and I didn't mean to tell her. I was thinking Kelly would want to tell everyone. It sort of slipped out before I knew it, but now I'm glad it did. I would hate for her to have said that stupid shit to Kelly," Max responded.

"That's true, but you know she sometimes talks first and thinks second. I know she wouldn't intentionally hurt Kelly."

"Intentional or not, Kelly doesn't need to be subjected to that dumb shit!"

"Relax, I know, but you didn't have to lose it on her. You could have just told her that wasn't cool and checked her response."

"I did. She needs to start thinking first and for folks to stop making excuses for her. She went off on me too. She didn't tell you that, did she?"

"Nawl, she sure didn't tell me that part. Little Miss Dede went off on Big, Bad Max?" Chan asked, amused.

"Yep, told me I thought I was Mother Teresa."

Chan laughed out loud.

"I don't know why you find that so entertaining, missy," Max noted sarcastically.

"I guess that makes you guys even now, so you let that shit go. Now when are we taking Kelly out? Should we say anything about the wedding?"

"Not yet. I'll tell her I told you guys. One day this weekend if everybody is available."

"Cool. Let me know. I'll talk to you later, Mother Teresa," Chan teased.

"Shut up," Max hung up.

Chan laughed out loud on the other end of the phone line and smiled inside about Dede sticking up for herself. She thought about how boneheaded a remark that was for Dede to make, but she knew Dede didn't mean any harm.

The girls got together a couple of weeks later. Whether Kelly wanted them to or not, they were spending the entire weekend with her. She was stuck with them. They were camping out and had already planned the slumber party. Each of them brought their favorite movie, their favorite meal, and a bridal book. They met at Kelly's house Friday evening and talked and ate all night. Kelly told them she picked the second Saturday in August. Since they had such a short time to prepare for the wedding, however small Kelly wanted it, they had lots of work to do, so they spent all day Saturday shopping and planning. They picked out the style of their dresses. They bought their shoes and the dress for Kelly's mother. They bought toasting glasses, centerpieces, maids' gifts, a garter, and a basket and pillow for the flower girl and ring bearer. They even bought the perfume they would wear. They bought something new and something blue. Kelly's mother had the something old. The most beautiful pair of antique pearl teardrop earrings. They even found a veil for Kelly. Although she hadn't chosen her dress yet, she thought the veil was so beautiful that the rest would have to evolve around it. They picked up invitations and accessories for the engagement party, and of course, they shopped just for the sake of shopping. That particular weekend, they gave new meaning to "shop until you drop."

Max was glad Kelly was having the wedding quickly. She would be able to wear the bridesmaid dress without getting a maternity size. She had to make sure she ate right and kept exercising so she wouldn't gain any excessive weight and fat. She decided she would tell them after the wedding. She didn't want to distract any attention from Kelly and her big day. There would be plenty time for her news.

While back at Kelly's place, continuing their slumber party, Chan told them she saw Marcus. "There was a Marcus sighting the other day, you guys," Chan said amusingly.

"Really?"

"Where?"

"Was this your first time seeing him since you guys broke up?" Dede asked.

"Yep, over in Jonesboro, at the pizza place we like. Todd and I went to eat after work," Chan responded.

"Did he see you?"

"Oh yeah, he definitely saw me."

"So?" Max urged Chan to continue.

"What'd you do?" Kelly asked.

"What happened?" Dede followed up.

They knew there had to be some kind of juicy story to accompany the announcement.

"Which one you want me to answer first?" Chan teased.

"All of them, girl. What happened?" Max answered abruptly and laughed.

"I was standing in line with Todd, and I looked and saw him about three or four people ahead of us. I knew he'd turn around eventually 'cause there was only one way in and the same way out. I was hoping he would either not notice me or not trip. Wrong on both accounts. He must have been waiting on the chance to curse me out and justify a reason for my leaving, as if his screwing around wasn't enough. He took one look at Todd, and that was the opening he needed to go all the way off on me. 'I knew I'd run into your trifling ass. So that's it, a brother ain't good enough for you no more? That's what's wrong with you bitches. Can't handle a strong black man, so you go running to the white boy trying to gold dig. I knew your ass wasn't shit from the start.'"

"Girl, no he didn't?" Kelly asked, exasperated.

"Yes, he did, and went on for a good minute. I was sitting there thinking, *How far into denial is this fool?* A sistah must not be good enough for him. At least not just one."

"So what did Todd do?" Dede asked.

"What was he supposed to do? If the need for fight or flight arose, he would have ran over me getting out of there. Shoot a crazed black man? And we were off duty too? Not worth the memorandum and the internal affairs investigation to shoot him," Chan teased.

"So you just stood there? Letting him rant and rave?"

"I was sort of in shock. I couldn't believe I was once crazy about this wild man I was witnessing. I was hoping he'd empty his tank, and I won't have to be subjected to his idiocy again."

"Right," Max laughed. "You fuck the brotha's brains out and then get mad cause he act like he ain't got no sense."

"So you saying this was my fault?" Chan asked defensively.

"No, of course not. Just wondering what you expected of someone with no brains."

"I don't know, but he cursed me like I stole something."

"Maybe he thinks you did. His manhood. Instead of tripping off his women and dissing the sisters, you just stepped. Walked away from that drama. How dare you?" Kelly interjected.

"He either never had it and was trying to find it through every woman he encounters or he sold it like he sold his soul in exchange for his charm. I was nothing but good to that man."

"I wonder what he was thinking in the first place?" Dede questioned.

"I really don't know. I don't care. You know what *I* wonder? I wonder why I ain't got no man yet. After all this time."

"If you stop being so damn picky, you'd have one by now," Dede shot out.

"Excuse me? Your ass ain't picky, and you're the same kind of manless, lonely, dejected heifa," Chan retorted.

"You're right about that. I'm damn sure manless," Dede laughed.

"I just wanna know what's the problem. And don't give me that in jail, gay, broke, or dead bullshit."

"Yeah, really, cause catching 'em ain't a problem. It's keeping one of them jokers that continues to elude me," Dede announced.

"Even the broke-down, not-prime-choice ones have the audacity to diss your ass these days."

"Right? What's up with that? You're not even all that interested in them, just kicking it for a while, and they up and quit you. Just leave you hanging."

"Well, maybe they felt you were playing," Max suggested.

"I wouldn't call it playing. It's just there were no fireworks going off from the start, but maybe it could have turned into something. I don't know. But you know what?

It doesn't matter if you sleep with them, don't sleep with them, give them attention, ignore them, share your feelings, hold back your feelings. Whatever the technique, it's been tried, tested, and *failed*."

"I guess we been using the wrong technique on the wrong man, the right technique on the wrong man, or the wrong technique on the right man. Either way, we've been missing the mark."

"I just wanna know when will I get the right technique on the right man?" Chan asked.

"But wait, this is the best part. After you spend all that time prepping for a relationship, helping them learn how to dress, act civilized in public, and treat a woman, and all the other heartache and dissing you endure, you guys break up anyway. You either catch him cheating or you just get tired of the drama. Then you see him with the next girl, treating her like he should have been treating you," Dede scoured.

"Ain't that the truth? But you know there's no need in getting mad at him or her. Just be happy he finally learned and we got another marketable brother out there. That way, the prospects don't continue to look so dismal."

"Yeah, and with more brothers to choose from, women might stop dissing each other due to slim pickings," Chan observed.

"And look at it this way. There's some woman going through the same stuff you went through, preparing him for *you*. So wait your turn. Patience and understanding, you'll get your complete brotha," Max reasoned.

"Shut up. Who asked for your philosophical point of view?" Chan teased.

"No need getting mad at the female who got your man. Why would you want him back anyway? He is no good for *you*! The history between you two is negative. You can't reverse that. All you can do is pray both of you have grown from the experience, and if your paths cross again, congratulate him on his graduation."

"Graduation? What graduation?"

"His graduation into manhood," Kelly responded cleverly.

The girls leaned back, laughing, and came up giving each other high fives.

"Girl, you are a nut. But that's the truth. We have got to stop sweating each other and giving these brothers all that ammunition against us," Chan agreed.

"There really are plenty of good men out there. I think both sexes have some kind of hang-up about the other. You either had some sort of bad experience or fed into the stereotypes and started generalizing the entire gender."

"Somehow we gotta let that go. Stop allowing our past to devour our future and see each man for who they are, not what they are—a man, like that last fool who hurt you so bad. That's not cool. That blanket mentality will doom every relationship encountered," Kelly surmised.

"I know. I'm happy you started hearing Josh when it was the right time," Max offered.

"Yeah, me too," Kelly responded dreamily.

"Oh, look at you," Dede teased.

"All innocent and in love. That's so cute," Chan chimed.

"Forget you guys," Kelly slammed.

They laughed again. Max wondered out loud about what else needed to be done for the wedding. "August is only a few weeks away. What haven't we covered yet?"

"I have to confirm the reception hall, and the invitations should be here next week. You guys will have to come back over so we can lick and stick and send them out as soon as possible."

"No problem. Is Pastor Lacy going to be available to officiate the wedding?" Dede asked.

"Yep, and of course, I still have to get my dress. When do you guys go for your measurements?"

"Next Saturday," Max answered.

"Oh yeah, and I have to take over the deposit for our honeymoon."

"Where are you guys going?"

"Zimbabwe, Africa, and a short island cruise."

"Kelly and Josh are getting married. Wow," Chan marveled.

"I'm glad someone else amongst us is finally getting married. Now I'm getting two for one," Max added.

# Wedding

It was a beautiful evening wedding. The girls wore knee-length soft pink knitted form-fitting dresses. The sleeves were long with matching faux fur at the cuff and around the collar. They had matching chiffon scarves that draped across their backs and wrapped around their arm. Later, at the reception, they would wrap them around their waist as a *sarong*.

The gentlemen had black Salvatore Ferragamo tuxedos with rose tapestry vests and soft pink ascot ties. Josh wore an ivory full-tailed tuxedo with an ivory shirt, ivory vest, and ivory tie and a light pink rose boutonniere.

The church was beautifully decorated with pink roses and white lilies all over it. The pews were looped in ivy laced with pink roses and a lily crossing the bow on the side of the pew. Candles were used to light the church and the aisle where Kelly would walk down. The runner for the bride to walk down was a soft pink to contrast the white rose petals the flower girls would throw.

Kelly's oldest brother, Ted, gave her away, and Max was the maid of honor. Dede, Chan, and Kelly's college friend Tracy were the bridesmaids. Josh's best man was Brian, his boy since fourth grade. The groomsmen were Mark his long-time homey, Tony Staten, and Kelly's coworker Ian because he so desperately wanted to be a part of Kelly's wedding.

Josh was thankful he had friends who would not feel slighted for being excluded from the wedding party. In fact, they were probably glad to not have to wear one of those binding, uncomfortable tuxedos. With the loss of Todd and Alex, Josh's friends who had died of AIDS, Josh had less of a dilemma filling his spots. Luckily, it was a small wedding court, and Kelly didn't have to do any choosing to fill her spots.

They tried to keep the wedding as small as they could, but the list kept growing. There were family and friends who would not miss this wedding for the world. Many of Kelly's relatives from out of town were coming, and the word spread to some of her college mates and buddies in California. Josh was a local boy, he grew up in Atlanta, and most of his family was still in the immediate and outlying areas. It was automatic that they would be there for the wedding. Before all was said and done, the couple ended up hosting about two hundred people. Besides, Mrs. LeBeau wasn't too thrilled about a tiny wedding for her only daughter anyway. She understood the time constraints but didn't feel they should limit their dream or fantasy. She let them know under no uncertain terms that money was not going to interfere with the planning.

It was a fairly traditional American ceremony. The ushers greeted the guest and escorted them to their seats. The mothers of the bride and groom were escorted down each outside aisle to light the six candles on each side of the unity candle near the center aisle. The wedding party filed in to the sounds of the keyboard and a duo singing "If This World Were Mine." While the choir boy and girl lit the candles around the church, and the ring bearer and maid of honor came down the aisle, the musician sang the gospel tune "His Eyes Are on the Sparrow." At the end of the song, the pastor said a prayer to bless the day and the ceremony.

By the time the organ was tuned up for "Here Comes the Bride," the crowd was already primed and almost to tears. The flower girls sprinkled layers of white roses to accentuate the bride's natural beauty and connection to God's creation. The music started, and everyone stood up to watch Kelly come down the aisle. She entered the doorway, and the lights dimmed as the candles lit the room, creating a romantic and religious surrounding.

She was so amazingly beautiful and glowing, the audience gasped. She wore a full-length fitted ivory dress filled with lace and pearls. It had a split in the front of the trumpet style dress, with a dropped bow above her buttocks that held her train. The train was about six feet long with live miniature pink roses attached to it. Her entire wedding displayed sensual elegance. She enveloped the sanctuary with the energy and euphoria she exuded. Josh took one look at Kelly and felt himself get weak in the knees. He thought to himself, *This girl always gets to me, but this is ridiculous. I feel like I'm about to fall the fuck out. Steady yourself, Josh.*

White tissue and handkerchiefs started popping out of purses and pockets. Others were fanning their faces directly at their eyes, trying feverishly to hold back the tears. Women were whispering and wiping around the bottom of their eyelids to keep the tears from pouring out and destroying their makeup.

You could feel the brightness of Kelly's smile behind the veil as well as the intensity of their joy filling every inch of the sanctuary. She glided down the aisle on earth's petals with such smoothness that it reminded you of one of those scenes from a Spike Lee movie where the actors appear to float toward the camera. When she reached the end of the aisle, the audience sat down, and the pastor began.

"Who gives away this woman?"

Kelly's brother stepped up on the left side of Kelly and cupped his arm around her elbow. "I give her away with love and respect, sir."

The pastor thanked Ted and gave his remarks for the union of the families. He then asked, "Who shall marry this woman?"

Josh, who was about two yards in front of Kelly, nearer the pulpit with the rest of the wedding party, stepped under the arches. "I will marry her, sir."

Ted walked Kelly up to the arches and gave her away to Josh. He took Kelly's right arm as Ted released her. Kelly and Josh faced the pastor, and Ted took his seat on the front pew next to his mother and brothers.

The pastor performed the ceremony according to the AME tradition. He had the couple turn and face each other and recite their vows. When the time came to place the ring on the bride's finger, nerves had taken over Kelly. She held her hand out, and it trembled so bad that Josh was not able to put the ring on it. With tenderness and understanding, Josh gently took Kelly's hand into his left hand to calm her and placed the ring on her finger. Everyone watched quietly with captivation and assent.

Josh repeated his vows, and they turned back to face the pastor as he continued the ceremony and pronounced them husband and wife. He gave the consent to remove the veil. Kelly had a tear dropping from the well of her eye, and Josh wiped it. The crowd oohed at the gesture as they wiped their own tears Josh forced from their eyes with his ideal attributes.

"You may now kiss the bride."

Josh thought this part would never come. He'd wanted to kiss Kelly since she walked through those doors seventy yards back. Anxiety was taking over him, knowing he had this beautiful woman at his side and he could only look at her. The only thing that kept him contained was the reality that the next act of passion would be with his wife—his K-D, baby, Mrs. Kelly Dawson. Josh gave her the most innocent yet passionate kiss allowed in a religious ceremony. Kelly blushed and consumed the full energy of his love. The crowd clapped and cheered, and they watched with admiration and support as the couple bequeathed the sanctuary.

The pastor announced, "I present to you Mr. and Mrs. Josh Dawson."

The couple honeymooned on an eleven-day safari and tour of Zimbabwe, Africa, and concluded it with a four-day cruise to Ocho Rios, Jamaica, and two nights on the island—two places that topped Kelly's list of things to do and places to go. They experienced and learned so much during their homecoming to Africa, and they knew their lives had been touched in such a way that neither of them would ever have the same perspectives or convictions. They spoke of the need for each and every person of African descent to experience this life-altering opportunity.

After the exuberant yet taxing trip to Africa, the cruise was the perfect solution for soothing, pampering relaxation. They enjoyed themselves and one another to no end.

They had decided to move into Kelly's place and rent out Josh's condo. While they were away, the girls and their friends and family emptied Josh's packed up place and moved him into their new home. Max, Dede, and Chan did their best, transforming the home into "his and hers" living quarters. Since men live and furnish bachelorhood to the fullest, most of Josh's belongings became guest room and family room furniture. Other items were interchanged, and they could visit the storage later and decide their own personal preferences.

After Kelly and Josh returned home, they gave them a week of space. They had left a banner hanging in the living room welcoming the couple to *their* new home. They left a note telling them not to call, just let their parents know they made it back safely, and everyone would contact them later. In the postscript of the note, the girls told Kelly she belonged to them the following Saturday.

That Saturday, Josh woke early and got out the house before the cackling hen fest began. He went for coffee and an early morning chess game with some of the coffee house regulars and met his golf buddies for a nine-o'clock tee time.

The girls picked Kelly up about eight thirty and went to breakfast. They opened their favorite mall in Buckhead. The security couldn't turn the key on the door fast enough for them to get in. The wildest part is they weren't the only ones waiting. A pretty decent-sized crowd had gathered outside the mall doors. Saks was having its semi-annual sale.

The girls were intent on getting at least one of the newest lines of trendy outfits, whatever it might be. By the time they came up for air, about three and a half hours had passed. Everyone had some sort of bag of something. All had fulfilled their goals to buy a new outfit. Everyone except Max. Several things had moved her to excitement, but the voice of reason overrode her whim. She knew soon, she would not be able to fit into anything and, for several months to follow, would not want to fit into anything binding. She held out.

They strolled the rest of the mall and picked up knick-knacks at the other stores along the way. At the other end of the mall, they went into the department store. Chan led them to the baby section. They started looking at the clothes and other items, adoring their miniature, cute size. No matter who you are, how tough you are, or what your image may be, a baby and baby clothing can tap that internal sweet, loving emotion. They wandered from rack to shelf, calling out to each other to look at the next darling item one of them had stumbled on. Each time, they aahed in unison at how cute it was.

Somewhere in time during the baby section excursion, Kelly became confused. She turned to find Chan and noticed she was at the cash register. She spotted Dede across the room and saw several items Dede had held up for observation was still in her arms. Kelly took off in pursuit of Max to find out whose shower they were shopping for and why she wasn't invited. By the time she arrived at Max's side, Max was standing in line one person behind Chan. At that same time, Dede walked up with her pile of pickings.

Kelly tapped Max's shoulder. "Okay, what's going on here?"

The girls sang out, "We're having a baby!"

Kelly looked at them quizzically from one to the other. "What? We are? Who? When?"

"Max. She's about five months now," Chan answered.

Kelly, Dede, and Chan all hollered at once, squatting slightly, and came up giggling and hugging. They took Max into their circle of love.

"Oh my God. You guys kept this from me all this time?" Kelly inquired.

"That's Max," Dede tattled with her hand pointed at Max. "She just told us last week, while you were honeymooning."

"What?" Kelly questioned with surprise.

"I'm just glad someone else in this family is finally having a child. Whew, that girl can keep a secret, can't she?" Chan chimed in teasingly.

"Well, that's for sure. Her better qualities can sometimes be a terrible flaw," Kelly agreed.

"Excuse me, I'm still here," Max interrupted.

Kelly laughed and hugged Max. "You know I still love you. Now excuse me, I've got some shopping to do." She turned quickly to retrieve the items she thought were too cute to leave on the racks.

Kelly and Josh lived in total bliss for several months. Nothing and no one could interrupt their happiness. They had great family and great friends and each other. But as the saying goes, when things are good, hang on and enjoy the ride. 'Cause into each life some rain must fall. The approaching storm wasn't too far from expectation, but its timing had to be the worst ever.

As the year neared its end and the holidays approached, Kelly took ill. She had gotten weak. Getting out of bed to go to work became a chore, and enduring the day was equally trying. Ultimately, Kelly had to go out on disability. Her body and mind needed rest. Kelly could no longer ignore the pains and signs of her illness. She was hospitalized several days before Christmas. Kelly appeared so weak and drained that you could literally see the life seeping out of her. She'd only lost ten pounds, but it was lost so quickly and her skin flaked, making anything sickly about her seemed magnified.

Max hated seeing Kelly this way, but nothing would stop her from visiting and loving her friend. She had started spending less hours at her restaurant due to her own fatigue. Max was due soon, at the end of December, and she felt like she would pop at any minute. She employed her waitress, Shawna, full-time now, and Tony came by each evening to help close and take the deposits to the bank. Max would go in and help out once or twice a week.

She spent all her free time at Kelly's bedside. When Kelly wasn't in pain or drugged into delirium, they talked and laughed endlessly. They regularly whispered about the cute young dreadlocked male nurse who attended to Kelly on the day shift. Whenever he came to check on Kelly, Max would step out of the way and position herself somewhere in the room to gaze at the nurse and his natural athletically built stature and flawless complexion. She marveled at the precision with which he handled Kelly, the equipment, and himself. The warm smile he'd give Kelly to comfort her obvious embarrassment of being so helpless was so genuine and full of life that one would conclude all is not lost with the younger generation. Max was thinking he was lucky she's happily married or she'd pull a Stella and get her groove back. She cocked her head to the side with intrigue and interest as she watched the nurse slash heartthrob leave the room.

Kelly laughed while she watched her friend in her devious act. "You really need to quit."

"That's him trying to steal me away from Tony. Can I help it if the fellas can't keep their eyes off my sexy, svelte body?" Max teased, rubbing the outline of her very large belly.

"Oh, that's what they call that shape now?"

"Hey, watch it. You know I'm sensitive about my roundness."

"Aw, I'm sorry, boo. Come get your hug," Kelly patronized Max.

"Okay then." Max hugged Kelly. "We'll just call it the 'expecting mother's glow' cause you know he wants me."

The two chuckled with their own understanding of how well they knew each other and could talk, smile, laugh, and cry about everything. Their unspoken moments were rarely awkward and simply appreciated.

Max had a big ole nine-pounds-and-eight-ounce juicy boy on Christmas day. The hospital had never seen so many well-wishers for mommy and baby at one time and with such short notice. This baby had an extra special blessing and was eager to enter the world and experience all it had to offer. The girls, Josh, and their families agreed to initiate Christmas at their homes early and then come to the hospital to celebrate with Kelly. Of course, Josh had been there all day, and a very swollen Max, Tony, and their parents who were spending the holidays with them waiting for the arrival of their grandbaby made it to the hospital around eleven thirty. Chan, her son Tyler, and her new boyfriend arrived shortly after Max. Dede came in next, a little after twelve o'clock, looking beautiful as ever, like she was about to do a photo shoot or a video or something.

She had not one but two very tall, way-handsome men in tow. Josh recognized one of them as JR Whitmore, the wide receiver for the 49ers. The other was Chad Hewitt, a Heisman candidate from Howard University. They were in town working on a promotional video for their endorser. Dede had a prime part in the video and was their host of sorts. More of Josh and Kelly's friends continued to file in and out throughout the day.

Around three thirty, Max got a real sharp pain and buckled over in agony. Tony rushed over to her to see what was going on. Scared Dede bolted out the door to find a doctor, nurse, janitor, or somebody. Anybody who could help her friend.

"Baby, you okay?" Tony asked tenderly, holding on to Max.

"Tony, I think it's time," Max said trying to straighten up.

"You do? How long have you been having pains?"

"For a while now. I didn't want to say anything," Max responded with labored breathes.

"You didn't want to say anything? Girl, are you crazy?" Kelly tried to chastise.

"You know she is," Chan answered. Dede arrived back to the room with a nurse or someone who looked enough like one to satisfy her panic and a wheelchair.

"Ma'am, you think you can sit in here?" the nurse asked. "I'm going to wheel you to the maternity ward."

Tony gave Chan their doctor's office and cell number. "Call Dr. DiBirio. Tell him we're at the hospital, and Max is going to deliver any minute now."

Tony followed closely behind and held Max's hand during the elevator ride. When they pushed through the double doors and approached the nurses' station, Tony saw Dr. DiBirio. Tony raced over to the doctor just as the doctor was receiving a call from Chan.

"Doc, Max is having the baby. She's right over there. If that's a call from here in the hospital, it's probably our friend upstairs. We were in the hospital visiting another friend when she got a real sharp pain." They began walking toward Max, and Tony continued, "She said she'd been having contractions for a while today."

Dr. DiBirio kneeled down on the side of Max and asked her questions regarding her contractions. "How far apart are the contractions? Are you feeling any wetness in your vaginal area?"

Max told him they were about ten minutes or so apart earlier, but now they seemed constant, subsiding a little but not really going away. The doctor ordered a bed and told them to get her to the labor room.

When Max stood to get in the bed, her water broke, and she was taken to the delivery room immediately. Within an hour and a half or so, Little Kelly was born. Tony was so elated. He held onto his son so long and hard that when Max finally got him in her arms, she fell asleep after her brief moment of cradling little Kelly. She had Kelly tucked away so tightly at her side with her arm wrapped around him that the nurse couldn't pry him loose when they rolled her into the recovery room.

The entire Christmas party waited anxiously at the nursery window for baby Staten to arrive. When Max was taken to her room, her guest visited her in shifts of two. Tony ran downstairs to the gift shop to get cigars, announcing, "It's a boy." They circled in and out her room for over an hour, congratulating them on their healthy, fine little boy.

Little Kelly was certainly fine. He was very responsive and aware and different than the other babies. His skin was already filled out and smooth. His bronze tan already glowing, not reddish and waiting for days or weeks of life to enhance his beauty. His eyes were bright and wide open since Max first held him.

Kelly couldn't come down to see the baby. Although she'd been feeling better, things hadn't gotten that great yet. Josh went back and told Kelly everything about the baby and the delivery that he could remember and showed her pictures. Their families divided themselves amongst visits to Kelly and the hospital's newest patients.

The next day, when Max was feeling better and could cautiously move about, she talked her doctor into letting little Kelly go up in his bassinet to see his godmother.

Kelly was overjoyed to see her namesake. The nurse raised the head of her bed so she could sit up and see Max's miracle. They both stared at one another, as if to have a secret conversation. Little Kelly smiled and wouldn't take his eyes off his heaven-blessed caretaker. Unspoken love and admiration felt nonetheless.

# Christening

LITTLE KELLY WAS GETTING CHRISTENED the fourth Sunday of the new year.

Kelly was getting better, but there was no certainty she'd be out the hospital for the christening or even feeling well enough to attend if she was released. Kelly's condition had stabilized, and her body was responding well to the antiretroviral therapy (ART). The doctors were hopeful she would continue to get stronger, and barring any setbacks, she would soon be able to go home. Kelly's viral load was reducing. Therefore, she was in a good position to return to her previous state of health.

The proud parents were up early Sunday, buzzing about the house and making a fuss over Little Kelly, making him look as angelic as they felt he really was. Peeking from the pure white christening outfit and blanket was his glossy, curly afro and his bright button-sized dark eyes. Kelly was a happy and calm baby. He seemed wise beyond his existence and always deep in thought. Whenever he was placed in his carrier or bassinet, he quietly observed his surroundings.

Max was really missing her friend. Although she had just seen Kelly two days ago, it felt more like a lifetime. It was one of the most important days in their life for sharing with family and friends, and her nearest and dearest would not be there to share it with them. While Max was visiting the hospital Friday, she didn't want to bring up the issue of Kelly going home or the christening so as not to put a damper on Kelly's spirits. Because Kelly insisted on smiling when things were at their worst, Max could never really tell how Kelly was feeling.

Max and Tony arrived at the church early, according to the directions of the pastor in the pre-baptismal meeting. Tony carried his son as Max walked ahead to scout for the best seating and positioning in the area designated for the baptismal candidates. As Max neared the front pew, she saw a wheelchair parked at the side of the pew, thus having the best seat in the house free of obstruction and the path of traffic. Max figured it was one of the church elders or a member who normally arrives early to avoid stumbling through the crowd in their wheelchair. Several steps closer, she made out the image of an additional body, sitting in the pew adjacent to the wheelchair. At that same instant, she realized she'd recognize that chocolate bald head anywhere. Max's eyes filled with tears, and she was racing down the aisle before even she was aware of what she was doing.

"Oh my God!" Max exclaimed as she embraced Kelly very purposefully.

No further words were spoken for several moments. Josh merely smiled at the homecoming and rose to shake Tony's hand when he arrived at their side. Max was virtually bawling. Now the day was complete. Everything would be perfect.

Max placed little Kelly's satin blanket across Kelly's lap and gently placed Kelly's godson in her arms. Their reunion was a mirror of their union. Only now, no barriers. The touch was electric. Max looked on with pride and joy. Suddenly, in sort of a panic, she began to search for her phone. This was the epitome of a Kodak moment. After several snaps, Max went to the restroom to fix her face. Soon, there was bound to be someone trying to snap her photo.

When Max returned, Little Kelly was sleeping, and Kelly was still closely watching the miniature miracle. No one bothered to move him, and he never stirred. The church had filled, and most of Max and Tony's guest had arrived and were chattering about. They too realized the seized opportunity and only came over to speak to Kelly and admire God's sleeping bundle. They recognized their chances to spoil him would be plentiful.

Kelly grew stronger with each day. Her ART therapy was finally working in her favor. Within one month after coming home, she spent more time out of bed and began taking short walks with Josh once a day or so.

By the time Kelly returned to work, she was feeling pretty well, but things weren't the same. She knew there was a lot going on around the office and that there would be some problems because Ian kept her abreast as best he could without dampening her spirits.

No insider reports could have prepared her for the mountain of work waiting on her desk or the sabotage Peter had cooking up. He and another engineer were assigned to pick up the slack and keep the general manager informed of important projects and any necessary executive decisions while Kelly was out. No crucial decisions or meetings were to be executed without the approval of Mr. Milstein, but Peter had made contact with three of Kelly's top clients and convinced them Kelly would be incapable of handling their needs to their expectations due to her debilitating disease and lost focus. According to Peter, Kelly had gotten selfish, and her attitude was that nothing and no one else mattered except her illness. "Besides, you don't really want to spend too much time with people like that anyway. You know there's still no solid information on how you can catch that stuff from someone," Peter offered openly in what he would later define as looking out for the best interest of the company and the clients.

The first week of Kelly's return, she made phone calls, set up meetings, and closed out files. She decided to work the weekend in order to clear up some of the clutter on her desk and make arrangements so she would only work in the office three to four days a week. She didn't want to overexert herself.

Ian and Josh gave up their weekend to come and help out. Kelly got overtime approved for Shelly, the floor receptionist, to come in on Saturday to assist her in tying up loose ends. They shuffled through mail, files, orders, proposals, and memorandums. They made phone calls and sent faxes. As the day wound down, Kelly continued looking for a couple of portfolios of her major clients that weren't in her cabinet or on her desk. She asked Shelly about them and requested her to look around for them when she had a free moment.

Shelly went straight to Peter's office. She figured he'd have them because she saw him meeting with some of their clients, the ITEC executives, while she was on a lunch break. Shelly was right. She found two of them in Peters' office. She gave them to Kelly.

"Oh, thanks, Shelly. Where'd you find them?"

"In Mr. Stan's office."

"Oh really? I wonder what he was doing with them. There was no urgent business pending on them. Unless something unexpected came up and Mr. Milstein had Peter handle it," Kelly wondered out loud. "I'll ask Mr. Milstein about it Monday."

"I sort of expected them to be amongst his things because I saw him having lunch or meeting with the ITEC suits last week," Shelly informed Kelly.

"Is that right?" Kelly asked, adding up incidents in her head.

"Yeah, he probably has the other one as well, but I couldn't find it anywhere in his office."

"And he leaves all these cases assigned to him on my desk incomplete but removes profiles that are off limits," Kelly concluded.

"And it's strange he couldn't complete the stack of work assigned to him but Mr. Sigher could," Shelly observed.

"Exactly. I wonder what he's up to this time," Kelly stated, becoming upset.

"Oh, you know what he's up to, Kelly," Josh interjected.

"He is such a snake. With things the way they are right now, Mr. Milstein may just let him take over my job." Kelly began to cry, and she slumped into her seat. "I don't think I can take on another battle, Josh. That backstabbing bastard probably swooped on them the moment I went on disability."

Josh bent down in front of Kelly and took one of her hands in his hand and her chin with the other and kissed her tears. He then took her head to his chest and stroked her hair for a moment. "You go ahead and get it all out now." Josh prepared to help strengthen Kelly. "This will be the last time you shed any tears where this bastard is concerned. No other moments of weakness for him to capitalize on. You know his type—lazy and greedy. Only energy he'll ever expend is to do dirt and whatever it takes to keep 'that black undeserving female' from continued success, but his evil and hate will forever keep him doing stupid shit. He doesn't want the ass whipping he's asking for. His arrogance continuously leaves him underestimating the opposition. His dumb ass would probably bring a knife to a gun fight. And *you* are gonna pull out the brigade. So toughen up, sister."

Kelly looked up and smiled in agreement and with understanding of Josh's intent. She thought to herself that Peter better hope she battles his ass in the office, quiet and quickly. If things actually got ugly, between Josh and her brothers, he *really* didn't want that ass whipping he was asking for. Kelly smiled, tickled by the vision of Peter cowering to those angry black men, all the while wondering what their problem was and all the while ignoring the fact that he pushed a button he didn't have to push.

"That's why I haven't gotten any of my calls returned. It's all coming together now." Kelly sobered up.

"You be sure to wear your stomping boots Monday," Josh kidded.

"I'm going straight to Mr. Milstein's office Monday. That way, he'll know exactly why I'm screaming and throwing shit when I see Peter."

Kelly arrived at work earlier than usual Monday. She wanted to make sure their computer system services connected the network to her home computer and that her laptop was operating with all the necessary programs. As soon as Mr. Milstein arrived in his office, Kelly was ten minutes behind him with a stack of files in her hand. She wanted to show Mr. Milstein the work Peter neglected over the period of her absence. She showed him the cases he left on her desk that she had managed to bring up to date and close out in just the short time she'd been back. She also showed the completion of the equal amount of work assigned to Jeff. She continued to tell him about the portfolios of her major accounts that disappeared from her files and were found in Peter's office. She informed Mr. Milstein she would probably be out the office most of the day meeting with her clients and straightening out the mess Peter had made.

When Kelly left Mr. Milstein's office, she stopped at her desk to get the files Peter had stolen and beelined to his office.

Shelly had also made it to work earlier than usual. She had an ulterior motive. She didn't want to miss any of the fireworks. She had already prepared and distributed coffee and the morning memos. She got a ringside seat and gathered her a stack of "busy" work to sink her head into in case someone looked over to see who was listening.

Kelly walked in and slammed the two files on Peter's desk. "So where's my other case, Peter?" Kelly asked firmly.

Peter tried to remain cool, but he hadn't expected Kelly to burst through his door and approach the situation with such force. He was used to the smiling, passive Kelly. "What case are you talking about, Kelly?"

"Look, goddammit, I don't have the time, patience, or interest to play these games with you. I've been vexed by smarter and more important assholes than yourself. Now are you gonna relinquish my case, or am I gonna have to tear this entire office up and have your car searched by security?" Kelly lit into Peter.

"Okay, listen, I can explain." Peter looked around, visibly upset and embarrassed his plan had taken this direction.

"I know damn well you can, but first, ass-up my case..." Kelly slammed his office door shut, still fussing.

Shelly could no longer hear their conversation, but she could still see Kelly digging into Peter. When she left his office, she was carrying three files. The receptionist smiled to herself.

Kelly went back to her office to settle herself down and prepare for the day ahead. To do some real work, where Kelly shined, meeting with clients and closing deals.

While Kelly was out, Peter was called to the carpet. He had gotten into a pissing contest and lost. Mr. Milstein believed the company would suffer greatly from Peter's work ethics. He was reassigned to the mailroom for an indefinite period. Security escorted Peter back to his office to remove all personal belongings and relinquish his parking and executive floor passes. He was suspended for a week with no pay and could quite possibly get demoted or fired.

# Dede

DEDE HAD BEEN GETTING QUITE a bit of work lately. There were lots of photo shoots and modeling assignments, but she especially enjoyed the consistent callbacks for parts as an extra with lines. Right now, she was up for a part in a new sitcom scheduled for the new season. If she got it, they would shoot the pilot soon in hopes of getting picked up by one of the major networks.

Today, Chan and Tyler were hanging out with Dede at a music video shoot. A trap music rap group was filming a video for their new single off their album. They planned to film for two days at the Olympic stadium and the underground and surrounding area. Dede had always refused to do music videos. She figured they'd do more to harm her career than to help it. She used her connection with F. Gary Gray, who was directing the video, to come on the shoot and learn some behind-the-scenes skills and let Tyler meet the group if possible.

It was an exciting day out, exhausting but good nonetheless. Dede managed to get exposed to quite a bit of information from being an observer.

Tyler was like a kid in a candy store. He couldn't believe all the work that went on to put those videos together. When he got to meet the group and the other stars and rappers who were hanging out on the shoot or making appearances in the video, he was definitely in heaven. They even took him to hang out with them closer to the actual filming for a while and talked with him between their breaks.

Dede, Tyler, and Chan left around seven o'clock in the evening after being there since five in the morning. They were so tired. Chan felt as if she'd actually done a full days' hard work. She took the opportunity to educate Tyler on the serious work involved in having that type of career. She also pointed out the various jobs, crafts, education, and dedication required in film and television. She warned him of looking in from the outside and getting caught up in the glamour of it all because, as he could see, there was much more to it. Dede told him the money doesn't really get big until you've survived the business for a while because all the activity he saw going on around there was paid for by the artists.

Chan was pleased some of the group members were telling him to keep up with his books and school because an education was crucial for handling the business aspect of the industry. When they got home, Tyler plopped down on the couch, clearly exhausted and excited at the same time.

"So you think you're too tired to go back tomorrow?" Chan asked, knowing the answer.

"Mom?" Tyler looked at her with an "I don't believe you're even asking that question" look.

Chan and Dede laughed. Dede then added her two cents. "I know I have to be careful what I ask for. It just about wore me out meeting everyone and getting familiar with their job assignments."

"Well, you better get some sleep now Aunt Dede cause we got an early wake-up call tomorrow," Tyler teased.

"Oh, you think you can hang, do you?" Dede splashed back.

"Most definitely. And the little cuties up there said they were coming back too."

"Oh, here you go." Chan rolled her eyes playfully.

"So the truth comes out. I should have known there was more to it than hanging out with your loving mom and auntie," Dede responded.

The doorbell rang. Tyler got up to answer it while Chan went to the kitchen to prepare a quick dinner, and Dede propped herself against the wall and glanced at the cable guide, scrolling the TV screen for the next movie. It was Tony, Max, and Little Kelly.

"Hi, Aunt Max," Tyler said, giving her a hug.

"Boy, look at you. How much bigger can you get?" Max inquired.

Tyler chuckled. He was used to the comments and teasing in amazement of his size. Tyler switched to Tony, giving him the male handshake and chest press.

Tony looked up at Tyler. "What are you, about six four now?"

"Yeah, something like that," Tyler responded in his gruff teenage voice as he turned to take Little Kelly into his arms. Tyler was good with children, and they all seemed to flock to him even though he tortures them most of the time. Little Kelly was still too young to experience Tyler's torment, so he was safe for now. Only hugs and cuddles.

Max and Tony walked further into the house and saw Dede first. They hugged and exchanged greetings. Chan came out the kitchen, hearing the familiar voices and looking for her baby. She quickly hugged Max and Tony and then took Little Kelly from Tyler. She kissed, hugged, and bounced him as he cooed with enjoyment. She propped him on her hip and went back to the kitchen to stir her rice for the smothered chicken she was simmering.

"What movies are coming on, Dede?" Chan called out.

"My all-time favorites, *Harlem Nights* and *Love Jones*. So do you want to laugh or love?" Dede put out for voting.

"Well, you know the men don't want the mushy stuff, and with the new addition, they aren't outnumbered anymore...," Max noted.

"It's *Harlem Nights*," Tony and Tyler concluded.

"I'll make the popcorn," Dede said, getting up.

"I guess I have red Kool-Aid duties," Max followed.

Chan checked the dinner and called Kelly. "Hey, girl. How you doing?"

"Good. What about you?"

"I'm fine. What are you up to?"

"Lying here in bed, getting ready to watch a movie. I just finished a proposal and climbed into bed. The movie will probably end up watching me. Josh is in the front, working on some stuff from the office. What are you doing?"

"You two. Always work, no play," Chan joked.

"Oh, there's some play going on," Kelly warned.

"I heard that, missy. Max, Tony, and Dede are here."

"Oh yeah? Where's my baby?" Kelly asked.

"Right here on my hip."

"Let me talk to him."

Chan put the phone to Little Kelly's ear, and Kelly talked to him in her baby voice. He looked out and around, listening to the sound coming from the phone and then gave Chan the RCA dog look. Chan laughed and put the phone back to her ear.

"So I guess you're in for the night, huh?"

"Yeah. I'm pooped, and Josh will be tied up for a while. See you in church tomorrow?"

"Uh, nope. We're going back to that video shoot in the morning."

"That's right. How was it?"

"Fun, interesting, and tiring."

"Oh good. Tell everyone I said hi and kiss boo-boo for me."

"All right, sweetie. Love you."

"Love you more. See you guys soon."

"Bye-bye."

# Episode

AFTER THAT LAST EPISODE AND hospitalization, Kelly had a very stringent ART regimen. Although she resented having to consume so much medication, she took them faithfully and at the required times. Through educating herself extensively about the disease, Kelly knew the virus inserts itself into the CD4 cells and could replicate and mature into infectious HIV throughout the body. If that happened, she knew her viral load would increase right along with the risk of complications.

That particular scenario is exactly what Kelly was now facing. She was having intense abdominal pains again and couldn't keep any food on her stomach lately. Kelly eked through the recent couple of days at work, then decided she'd better take off and go to the doctor.

She first wanted to visit her mom and talk to her about some of the things she was thinking about her current situation. She told her mother of the pain she was experiencing and that she feared her kidneys were failing because she virtually stopped having the need to go to the restroom.

"Baby, you better get to the hospital and see what's going on," Mrs. LeBeau instructed worriedly.

"I'm going today, Mom. I just wanted to come and talk to you first. I believe I may be getting pretty sick now, and if it is kidney failure, I don't know if there is much they can do before my system starts shutting down and things get real bad."

Mrs. LeBeau didn't really want to hear or accept the information Kelly was offering her. "Baby, don't talk like that. If it is your kidneys, don't we have other options? Can't we get a transplant or something? You sound like you're giving up."

"I don't know. We'll see, Mom, but I also don't want to be alive vegetating. Just existing with no life in me. I want to talk to you, warn you, while I'm reasonably healthy, that things could change drastically, and I want you to be prepared for it."

"We'll talk about that if it happens."

"No, then it'll be too late. We have to talk now, face realities. I want you to stay strong, Mom. Understand I'll be better when all this is over, and I don't want you to start giving up trying to visit me when I'm gone. I'll visit you from time to time. You have to stay here and help take care of my bigheaded brothers. You still have more weddings to attend and some grandchildren to spoil."

Tears welled up and fell from Mrs. LeBeau's eyes. "Kelly, this is all too much for me right now. Can't we wait to see what your doctor says today? I'll go with you," Mrs. LeBeau pleaded.

"Mom, everything will be fine. Don't worry and upset yourself. Josh is going to meet me at the hospital when he gets off, and Max is going to take me. You stay here and relax. I'll call you this evening, okay? I love you, and we'll do something this weekend."

Kelly returned home and waited for Max to pick her up. When Kelly arrived at the doctor's office, he ordered a series of test to check her CD4 and viral load. He admitted Kelly due to the urine and bowel blockage in an attempt to cleanse and nourish her body. When Kelly got to her room, she called Josh and told him she was being admitted and not to rush over because the doctor was running test and it might be a while. She then asked the nurse to get Max, and she called her mom and told her the same calm story in an attempt to alleviate her worrying.

"Mom, I'm staying in the hospital a couple of days for testing and cleansing. Tell Mack or Ted to bring you by here tomorrow, and we'll see when I get to go home. Get some rest, and I'll see you tomorrow."

Kelly's T cell count had dropped to under two hundred, and her viral load increased. Her immune system was considerably weaker and unable to fight for her. She had developed Kaposi's sarcoma. She began to sicken due to HIVAN, a kidney disease that left her weak and fatigued and short of breath. It could no longer filter out bacteria and eliminate waste. She had long since talked with Josh about her feelings on allowing any medication or treatment that kept her breathing but left her feeble and decrepit. She did not want to slowly enervate. They opted not to have the chemotherapy. She felt it would only make her look and feel worse and be ineffective in sustaining any kind of vibrant life.

Kelly asked when she could go home, and the doctor essentially told them she could whenever she liked. He explained some of the effects they could expect to happen during the course of the cancer and kidney failure and other things that could develop. He also said it was likely they would need home health care, and the probability of falling into a coma was very strong. Kelly would find herself on morphine for the excruciating pain and, without treatment, was expected to live no longer than six months.

Josh took his wife home and tried to prepare himself and the home for the months to come. He made arrangements for a hospital bed and supplies and a home-care nurse, and he took a leave of absence. He tried to prepare his mind for the inevitable and the traffic of family and friends that would engulf their home.

Josh spent just about every waking moment with Kelly. He took his wife for tender walks and personal field trips when she had the strength for it. His will kept her stoic. He made sure she was dressed handsomely yet comfortably. Through home remedies and authorized dermatologic treatments, he battled the ashen skin her viscera could no longer replenish or had destroyed. Her beauty and vitality never exhausted in Josh's eyes.

Josh couldn't sleep at night for watching Kelly. He feared she'd slip into a coma or may need him and he wouldn't hear her. He clung to her every breath. He slept in the morning or napped throughout the day while the nurse tended to Kelly and visitors passed through.

One night, while Josh and Kelly were watching a movie, he sat at her bedside stroking her now thin, fine wavy hair, and Kelly reached for Josh's hand.

"Baby, I'm tired," Kelly whispered.

"You want me to stop the movie? Go ahead and rest. We'll finish it tomorrow."

"Not that. I'm tired of hurting. I'm tired of being a burden. I'm tired of not helping myself, and I'm tired of waiting. Waiting to die is a worse feeling than any of the pain I'm experiencing."

"I know, sweetie. I hate it for you. But you do know you're not a burden. I'm certainly not tired yet. If you have any energy left in you, don't give up yet. I'll take care of us both," Josh begged, refusing to cry.

"Honey, there's nothing to give up. All the worth I am to you, anyone, or life is gone. I need to go somewhere I can be more valuable," Kelly spoke irrefutably.

Josh simply held her hand, and they continued to watch the movie. Kelly fell into a fitful sleep that night. When morning came, she asked Josh to call Max and have her bring Little Kelly over as she called Tracy and talked with her for hours. She knew her mother and brothers would come by sometime during the day. She visited and spoke with all her house callers with more energy than usual. They were glad to see her feeling better and had hopes of her improvement.

Kelly fell asleep earlier than usual that evening. Josh and the nurse figured she tired herself expending all that energy with everyone. She slept for hours without waking between nods.

Josh watched her as usual. He dimmed the lights, turned off the TV, tuned the radio to an easy listening station, and lowered the volume. Lou Rawls was crooning:

*Talkin' 'bout groovy, groovy*
*Groovy, groovy people*
*Now baby, oh darlin', we don't have to put*
*up*
*With them jive-time folks no more*
*Let's pretend that we're not at a-home*
*When they come knockin', knockin' on our*
*door*

Josh knelt down beside Kelly's bed, held her hand, and laid his head at her side. As if the atmosphere and gentle touch spoke to her, Kelly turned her head toward Josh.

"I love you," Kelly spoke, low and crisp.

"I love you more," Josh responded, sincerely and unrehearsed.

They continued to lie there in that same position, quiet, each marveling at having someone to love so deeply. Josh fell asleep, and Kelly never woke up.

# Funeral

Josh, Mrs. LeBeau and her sons, Max, and Little Kelly sat on the front pew of the church, numb and sobered by the obsequies going on around them. Many of Kelly's other family members sat around them and immediately behind in the next pews.

Josh sat still, staring at his wife in the casket. He was coherent and aware of his surroundings, but his only focus was to keep watch of his wife until it was no longer possible. Max sat in her space, holding on tightly to Little Kelly, her only grip for keeping herself together. As if he could sense the need to be strong for his mother, Lil Kel never fretted. He let his mom hold on, and he observed everyone's sadness. Kelly's brother Ted twiddled his fingers and wrung his hands together, trying to stay in tune with the course of the service. Mack sat with his head buried in his hands the entire time, trying to tune out the progression of the service. His realization that his baby sister is gone and the awareness of everyone expressing their grief was more emotion than he cared to experience. Her youngest brother sat motionless. The most surprising expression was that of Mrs. LeBeau. She sat poised and simply rocked. Everyone expected she would be the one to take it the hardest, losing her only daughter and baby. No parent ever expects to out-live their child. People thought Mrs. LeBeau would com-pletely break down at the funeral. Her sons subconsciously hoped she would lose some sort of control so they'd have any distraction to bring them out of their trance. It never happened. They had to save themselves.

When the usher guided the mourners to view the body and exit the sanctuary, they passed the family, giving their condolences, and embraced the immediate family. Kelly's college buddy Tracy returned to town for the services as well as several other old buddies and college mates. Few of the mourners seemed to hold themselves together as well as Josh and Mrs. LeBeau. They were last to say their goodbyes to Kelly as everyone gathered in the parking lot to caravan to the internment.

Max didn't join the family at the seats reserved for them in front for the burial. She gave Little Kelly to Tony and stood behind with everyone else. She literally began to feel her strength vanishing. While the official spoke and sprin-kled flowers on top of the casket, an involuntary moan of anxiety seeped from Max as she held on to herself, feeling the tightening and pressure of her insides and the buckling of her knees. Her outburst set off a symphony of sobs. She regained movement in her legs and walked away from the crowd to a nearby tree strong enough to hold her up. Chan and Dede followed to console their friend and share their lament. They found a bench and held on to each other.

Over to the side, a few feet behind them, they could hear heaving and uncontrollable sobbing. Tracy was over there, literally sick. She had long since left the crowd and was trying to grip her agony. Although many miles apart, she and Kelly remained really close and talked regularly. She needed, expected, and depended on their tradition. The reality of her sister-friend connection severed, sickened her. The fiber of her being ached with sorrow. Her confidant, bearer, and provider of her college memories and so much more was gone.

The girls looked over to the source of their distraction. They bubble-gummed themselves together and got up in unison. They felt awful to see Tracy suffering alone. All the way in another state, and her actual connection to the city was being lowered into the ground. Chan gave her napkins, and Dede held her hair back and helped wipe her face. Max stepped in and held Tracy tight as her body hiccupped with grief. They found strength in numbers and eventually headed back toward the burial site. The internment was over. Everyone was going to their cars. Tony waited at the car for Max. She came over with Tracy and told him she would ride with Tracy because she was there alone, and they'd meet him at Mrs. LeBeau's house.

Josh had all the hospital remnants and illness reminders removed from the house before the funeral. He didn't want to come home and have the memories of the recent weeks override their more pleasant times together. When he returned home from the funeral, he basked in the vivacious memories of Kelly. There were photos around the home of them and everyone close to them. Pictures from the times when they were platonic friends, when they grew to lovers and friends, on to their wedding day and the rapture that followed.

The ecstasy of having Kelly in his life was an inner strength to Josh, but he couldn't bear the unhappiness he felt being in their home without her. He began to pack some of his things and many of the photos Kelly had warmed the house with. He decided to spend a few days alone at one of the places where he and Kelly would go to get away.

Josh made a couple of phone calls and began to change the message on their answering machine, leaving information on how to contact him later. Before he recorded his message, he pushed the outgoing announcement button one last time.

The jovial voice of Kelly announced, "Hi, you've reached the Dawson residence. And guess what, we're not talking to you right now, but we will. If you speak after the beep."

End

# About the Author

REGI IS A NATIVE OF Los Angeles, retired law enforcement officer, and graduate of USC Annenberg School of Communications. This is her first published book, as she realizes her dream of being a writer and reflecting on her journey that has always led to writing. Regi has written poetry, short stories, speeches, and pilots. Her inspiration for *Groovy People* was to capture the positive aspects of the majority in her community, shed light on the seriousness of HIV, and shift the focus of stigmatization. Her writing journey has included creative writing projects, stage performances of her work, and career advances, via authoring policies and agency standards. Her desire is to create works that will entertain, educate, uplift, and inspire.

CPSIA information can be obtained
at www.ICGtesting.com
Printed in the USA
LVHW091758220121
677210LV00035B/415

9 781648 014017